NOBODY NEEDS TO KNOW

in memory of my dear friend,
Keith Evans

Tanya Farrelly

NOBODY NEEDS TO KNOW

ARLEN
HOUSE

Nobody Needs to Know

is published in 2021 by
ARLEN HOUSE
42 Grange Abbey Road
Baldoyle, Dublin 13, Ireland
Phone: 00 353 86 8360236
arlenhouse@gmail.com
arlenhouse.blogspot.com

978–1–85132–229–9, *paperback*

Distributed internationally by
SYRACUSE UNIVERSITY PRESS
621 Skytop Road, Suite 110
Syracuse, NY 13244–5290
Phone: 315–443–5534
Fax: 315–443–5545
supress@syr.edu
syracuseuniversitypress.syr.edu

Typesetting by Arlen House

cover painting 'Vaudeville Nights'
by David Sweet
is reproduced courtesy of the artist
www.davidsweet.co.uk

CONTENTS

NOBODY NEEDS TO KNOW

Between the Lines

Last night they took mam away. Auntie Phyllis made the call, said it was for her own good. It's not the first time mam's been in; but this time they reckon she's a grade four, which means she has to be watched in case she does something.

Phyllis has been bustling round our house for a week now. She's the one who's speaking to the media, the one who's been liaising with the embassy, making all the arrangements to bring Gemma back home.

Mam has stopped speaking. I hold her hand and she sits, listless. Water leaks from the corners of her eyes, even when she makes no sound. She's stopped combing her hair, stopped putting on makeup. She looks different; younger and older at the same time. Her skin scrubbed clean and the absence of the black flicks at the corners of her eyes give her a less feline look – more like me than Gemma.

Phyllis comes every day. She talks to the nurses, asks where they're from. When mam's out of earshot, she asks them whether she's eaten anything. She eyes the puddle of ice cream in the bowl and questions them about mam's progress.

There's a television in the room. It's always on. The nurses turn it on, I think, to cancel out the silence. Mam doesn't watch TV. I've brought in her sketchpad and a set of pencils. Apparently though, I did too good a job sharpening their tips, and so the nurses removed them. No sharp objects, they say. Knitting needles are out too, I can't even leave a pair of tweezers. Crayons, the nurses tell me, it might be nice if mam had a set of crayons.

Nobody has mentioned Gemma to mam, not since she came in here. Phyllis snatches up the remote control and changes the TV channel every time Gemma's face appears on the screen. I've never seen that picture of my sister before. They must have got it from among her things – from the backpack that's accompanied her around Europe. She's wearing cut-off denims and a pink vest. Her skin is tanned from so much time spent outdoors. Her blonde hair is scraped back into a ponytail and she's smiling at whoever was behind the camera.

Mam didn't want Gemma to go on that trip. She'd nearly had a fit when she mentioned it. She'd only conceded because Kevin was going too. She'd be safe, Gemma had insisted, with Kevin. And she was – except they'd split up after only two weeks traipsing round Valencia, but there was no mention of that in the postcards she sent from Krakow, Budapest, Sofia ... We only found out she'd been travelling alone when we were contacted by the police. Naturally, mam told them about Kevin. He was questioned, but of course he had nothing to do with it. I knew that from the get-go. No matter how much Gemma got up Kevin's nose, he wouldn't hurt her. Not even if she deserved it.

I'm off school. Auntie Phyllis says it'll be time enough to go back after the funeral. We still don't know when that will be, don't know when Gemma will be returned to us –

when her remains, as they say, will be repatriated. I've already begun to picture Gemma in the coffin. I've taken out her blue dress, laid it on her bed, ready to take to the funeral home. I've matched it with a pair of silver sparkly sandals, and the blue drop earrings that mam bought her for her eighteenth birthday. They will dress her, like a doll, lift her arms and head and ease the dress onto her still body. They'll cover any bruises with foundation, though mostly the parts that are hurt are hidden. I know this because I've overheard the phone calls. Listened to Auntie Phyllis saying things like 'she wasn't ...' and then trailing off as the voice at the other end confirms that she was. I can tell from the way my aunt closes her eyes, and clutches at her throat, voice constricting. 'Poor child. Poor child.' And me squatting by the banisters.

That day, after the police had left and the three of us sat there crying, Phyllis asked about contacting dad. Mam had looked up, sharply, said she didn't know where *that man* was, that it wouldn't surprise her if he was found in a ditch. At that, we both started crying again, and Phyllis got up to make another pot of tea.

I couldn't get Gemma out of my head, the idea of her lying in a mortuary in Romania; cold, naked, a tag on her toe like those corpses they showed in the *CSI* series. She'd be shut up in a fridge until somebody came to claim her. It ought to be my father who did that, oughtn't it? God knows he'd done nothing else only bring us into the world, but mam was adamant that he wouldn't see us out of it – not any of us.

I'd asked Gemma once if she remembered him. She was five when he left, I was two. She shrugged and said she remembered a visit to the zoo. He'd bought her a monkey on a swing, which I apparently broke. 'Was I there?' I asked. She'd narrowed her eyes and thought hard. 'I think so,' she said. 'I think we got you in one of the enclosures.' We'd fallen round laughing then. We were eating ice pops sitting on the garden wall. I still remember the taste on my tongue, of ice cream and tangy orange.

In the mornings, I take Mufti, Gemma's spaniel, down to the beach. I sit on a rock while she sniffs the seaweed washed up on the strand, leave Phyllis cleaning imaginary dirt from the carpets. The floor has never seen more vacuuming than it has in the past week and the rooms are barely lived in.

That first morning, after we'd had the news, I'd gone down to the beach whilst the house swarmed with people. Neighbours poured in the front door. They came with mass cards, casseroles, words that consoled no one. Was it any wonder that mam stopped talking? But not before she cleared the lot of them out with her screams. I doubt there'll be anyone venturing over to the house for a while now. Of course, they didn't know about mam's episodes; her bouts, as they call them, of depression. Sometimes the world is too harsh a place for mam. She doesn't know how to be in it.

The neighbours had eyed me, stroked my hair, patted my shoulder – commented on the fact that I was so like my sister. The only thing me and Gemma have – had – in common is that we've got two eyes, arms and legs like everyone else on our street. And what right had they anyway to stroke and paw me? I'm not a child; I'm seventeen. I took the dog's lead from the kitchen and disappeared out the back door leaving mam and Phyllis to the carrion seekers. It was my sister who was dead, not me.

When I got down to the strand I stooped and unclipped Mufti's lead. She ran ahead, stopped to smell something dead: a crab, washed up on the sand. She poked it with her paw. Then jumped back and crouched down on her forelegs waiting for it to move. I took out my phone, scrolled through the contacts until I came to Kevin's number. 'On the beach,' I wrote. 'Can you meet me?' It was less than fifteen minutes later when I heard the Kawasaki come under the bridge. I clipped the lead onto Mufti's collar and headed toward the car park halfway along the strand.

I lifted my hand when I saw him coming towards me. Blue t-shirt, leather jacket swinging open, helmet in his right hand. Up close his eyes were red from too much crying. 'You heard?' Of course he'd heard. The police had surely been in touch with him. And it was plastered all over the telly. We began walking, Mufti running before us.

'I should've gone with her,' he said.

'You did.' I eyed him sideways, took in the dark circles under his eyes. He looked like he hadn't slept in weeks.

'We parted in Valencia ... and I figured she'd quit. Come back home, like I did.'

'What happened?'

'Nothing. Stupid row.'

'What about?'

Kevin shrugged. 'Can't remember. We were driving each other crazy.'

We picked our way over the rocks, climbed up on the old harbour wall. He put his helmet down between us.

'How are you holding up?' he asked. 'How's your mum?'

'I'm ok, kind of numb.' Mufti barked up at us from below. 'Mam's not good. You know what they were like, two peas ...'

'I should go see her.'

'You, why?'

He looked at his hands, bit on a nail. 'Because I feel like it's my fault.'

'Don't be stupid,' I said. 'How could it be your fault?'

He stretched his legs out, let them fall back to kick the harbour wall. 'It was my idea, the trip, and if I hadn't left

...'

'Yeah? Well, maybe if you hadn't gone to begin with,' I shot back. Mufti was still barking, causing a racket on the strand. I jumped down from the wall, landed badly on one ankle. Ignoring the pain, I stumbled furiously back the way we'd come. Behind, I heard Kevin hurry after me. A few more paces and his hand on my arm waylaid me. 'What are you getting so mad for?' I walked on, wondered if he was really that thick. Maybe he was. Maybe Gemma had deserved him.

The visitors had dispersed when I returned to the house. Mam was in her room, quiet now after screaming the house down. Phyllis said she'd called the doctor. She was busy scrubbing the floor in the living room. The dustpan was next to her full of bits of broken crockery; a gloopy brown liquid dripped down one wall, bits of carrot and potato clinging to the paintwork. The idea of mam flinging the dish at the wall made me want to laugh. I wondered how many of the do-gooders had been covered in casserole before they'd managed a sideways dive to safety. I bet they weren't long scurrying out the door after that.

The doctor gave mam Valium. He eyed me and asked Auntie Phyllis if she thought I might need something too, just a small dose to get me through. I told him I was fine, but he wrote the script anyway and left it with Phyllis, just in case. The Valium didn't help mam, instead it made her withdraw further into herself. She stayed in her bedroom for days, and then I went up to find her gone, but she'd strayed only as far as Gemma's room. When I looked in, I saw the form in the bed, the top of her head just visible beneath the duvet. Mufti was curled on the end of the bed like she did when Gemma was here.

It was when Phyllis walked in to find mam staring at the pile of pills collected in her palm that she called the doctor again. She sat on the edge of the bed and tried to get mam to look at her. Mam just kept looking at the pills, ignoring

Phyllis's questions about how many she'd taken. It turned out she'd only taken three, not enough to harm her. Looking at her, how shut off she was from the world, I began to wonder if I shouldn't take that prescription that Phyllis had put in her purse and have it filled immediately. Phyllis took mam's hand. 'Fi,' she said. 'You need to think of Aileen.' I came into the room then. 'Don't worry about me mam. I'm alright,' I said, kneeling before her. But mam just looked at me blankly, and when they came to take her, she made no protest.

I've brought mam her pastels, rather than the nurses' suggestion of crayons. What do they think she is – a child? I hate the condescending way that they talk to the patients here, like they've lost their marbles altogether rather than temporarily misplaced them.

When Phyllis isn't here, mam and I sit in companionable silence. I read or study, she sits. Sometimes I ask her if she's watching the TV, and when she shakes her head I switch it off so that mam and I can be alone without the danger of Gemma's face appearing above us. But even with the TV off Gemma is still here. Her presence stronger even than it was when she was alive. She's in mam's silence and in my thoughts. I can't mention what I need to talk about most, not to mam, not like this, and I wonder if we'll ever be able to talk about it.

Today when I arrive Mam is in her counselling session. They've changed the time and, of course, nobody thought to tell me. In fairness to them they seem quite lax about visiting hours, and so I sit and wait for her to return. I'm pleased when I notice some of the pastels scattered on mam's sketchpad. I move them to the side and open the book. She's filled it with drawings – drawings of a blonde-haired girl – drawings of Gemma. The face is not as sharp as it would have been if mam had been allowed to keep her pencils, but it's definitely her. In one, her hair is pulled back and she's wearing the pink vest from the photo on the TV, and even though mam seems to stare through rather than at the screen she's obviously committed it to memory.

That trip, if only mam had insisted she couldn't go. In fairness though, Gemma had just turned twenty and so she could have gone anyway. She didn't need anyone's consent, but she wouldn't have – not if she'd known how it would break mam's heart. Mine was already broken.

Last night Auntie Phyllis sat me down, asked me how I was doing. For once she wasn't cleaning or on the phone, and we sat there, her in mam's armchair, me curled in a ball on the sofa trying to read a book that belonged to my sister. I'd found it on her locker, a page turned down at the corner where she'd stopped. She'd bought herself a Kindle before the trip, and I wondered if she'd downloaded this book, or if she ever finished it. The book is *Rebecca*. It's about a young woman who marries a rich man whose wife is dead – and the young woman knows she can never live up to Rebecca. That's how I feel most of the time about Gemma.

I sit now in mam's room and try to concentrate on the book, but my mind keeps drifting. It drifts, as it often does, to the first time I met Kevin. Billie Sanders' family was having a garden party to raise money for kids in Zambia. It was something they did every year; there was a barbecue and a tent where they invited local musicians to play in aid of the charity. Billie and me had been taking ukulele classes together and she'd persuaded me and two of the others in the class to form a quartet to play at the event. Everyone who went would give a five euro donation.

Billie's older brother, Bren, was the lead singer in a band and they were the headlining act for the night. Kevin O'Rourke, it turned out, was the drummer. We began talking in the queue for the barbecue, and stood chatting about music until Billie dragged me away saying we were up after the interval. 'Do you know him?' I asked Billie, glancing back. 'Who, Kev?' She shrugged. 'Yeah, he hangs out with Bren. They think they're the next Coldplay.'

I met him again shortly after that. I was standing outside the Sanders' place waiting for Billie to get her ukulele when the Kawasaki came up the drive. Kevin smiled as he took the helmet off. 'Well, if it isn't the ukulele lady,' he said, grinning. He got off the bike, opened a box on the back and took out a bunch of fliers. He handed me one and on it was a picture of the band and an advert saying they were playing in the local GAA grounds the following Wednesday. 'What do you think?' he said. I nodded. 'It looks great,' I said. 'Would you be up for it?' 'I'd love to, but I'll have to see.' I didn't mention that I was under age, although I assumed he knew. I was, after all, in the same year as Billie.

When Gemma came across the flier in my stuff, she said we should go. 'Yeah, maybe,' I said, telling her nothing about Kevin. 'Do you think I'd get in?' Gemma smiled. 'Leave it to me sis.' She sat me down at her dressing table that evening and applied my makeup. I had to admit, she did a great job. She didn't overdo it like some of the girls did when they were trying to get into clubs. 'Wow! Just look at those lashes,' she said, standing back to admire me. She even lent me her pretty yellow dress with the butterflies, but none of it was enough to keep Kevin O'Rourke's eyes off my sister who flirted without even knowing.

Mam gives me a slight smile when she comes back from counselling. I put my book down and get up to give her a hug, but she still feels brittle when I put my arms around her. She raises her hands but they barely touch me. 'I see you've been drawing,' I say. Mam glances at the sketchbook, opens the pages as if she's forgotten maybe what she's drawn there. 'I don't want to forget her face,' she says. 'You know it's been three months since we've seen her.' I nod, wonder how much I should say in relation to Gemma. 'I met Kevin,' I say, 'at the beach the other day. He said he'd come to see you.' Mam bristles. Whatever she's been talking about with the counsellor it's done something to wake her senses. 'Why wasn't he there?' Mam says. 'Where was he when ...' 'They fought. Gemma decided to go on alone. He didn't want her to.' I don't know this. I'm putting words in Kevin's mouth. All he said was he didn't think she'd go on ... but I have no idea if it would have made a difference. 'It wasn't Kevin's fault,' I say. 'He thought she'd call an end to the trip same as he did ...' 'Well – it's ended now alright,' mam says. 'If that boy –'

The door opens and Auntie Phyllis rushes into the room, her eyes going immediately to the blank TV screen. 'I've just heard it,' she says. 'On the car radio. You'd think they'd have bloody called me ...' She crosses to the locker, breathless, and picks up the remote control. She stops then, shaking, to tell us the news before we hear it as she did. She takes both our hands and we stand there like we're about to begin a game of ring-a-ring-a-roses, like Gemma and me did when we were little. 'They've got him, Fi,' she says. 'Arrested him last night.' Mam looks at her, blankly. 'Who?' I say, my throat constricting. Phyllis lets go of our hands and the TV fizzes to life. We stand around listening to how water charges are being scrapped, about how hospital waiting lists have doubled, and then we see him. Right next to the usual picture of Gemma, the screen split down the middle. He's young, about Gemma's age. *A man has been arrested for the murder of Irish backpacker Gemma Halvey*, the announcer says. Mam grasps my hand. I glance at her, at the tears spilling down her face. As Phyllis's phone goes off, I feel like I'm choking. She rushes from the room and I want to follow, but mam's hand has tightened round mine and we stand there, fingers entwined, staring at the screen at the man who killed my sister.

DING DONG JOHNNY

'You know you could die in this place. Ding-Dong-Johnny could take an axe to that door, bash both our heads in, and not one neighbour would fuckin' hear.'

It had been going on for at least half an hour; intermittent roars starting off sing-song-like only to convert, in seconds, to a bellowing crescendo.

'A quarter past bloody one,' Roz said, throwing the covers back and swinging her bare legs onto the floor.

'What are you doing? You're not going out to him?'

'Damn right I'm not,' she said, pulling on her robe. 'I'm ringing the guards is what.'

Ding-dong-Johnny-Johnny-whatsit-ding-dong-day, the strange nursery rhyme, accompanied Roz's form out the door. I sat up and turned on the bedside lamp. 'Turn it off,' she hissed. 'We don't want him knowing we're here.' *Ding-dong-Johnny-Johnny ...* The voice was getting louder, brasher. It felt like he was in the goddamn spare room. I opened the door to make sure he wasn't, was relieved to see the usual mess. 'Fuck's sake.' I pulled on a t-shirt and followed Roz into the front room.

'Yeah, look, I'm ringing about a neighbour. He's been shouting non-stop for the past hour. Sounds like he's having some kind of meltdown. I don't know, some weird nursery rhyme, then he starts into this string of obscenities. Listen, you'll hear him yourself if I go out to the hall.'

We sat in the dark and waited for them to come. 'What the hell is he saying anyway?' I said. Scrunch of tyres on gravel had us out of our seats. 'Fair play,' Roz whispered, ducking the headlights on the wall. 'That was fast.' I went into the hall, waited for the buzzer to go – 'Do you hear that,' I whispered to the uniformed pair in the porch. *Ding-dong-Johnny* ... was going at full volume. The reply was running steps on the stairs outside, a bang on the door opposite, and all went quiet. Roz and I jostled for space like players in a rugby scrum, ears fixed against the door.

'Tommy. Are you alright in there?'

Silence.

'Are you alright, Tommy? We heard shouting?'

The door opened. 'What do you want?' In the voice not a trace of the hysterics of the moment before. 'I didn't call you. Did someone call you?'

A struggle as Roz and I tussled for the lock. 'Don't,' I whispered, but she threw my hand off and flung open the door.

'Yeah,' she said. 'I called. You've been screaming in there for nearly an hour. Have you any idea what time it is?'

Roz. Hot-headed Roz. I pulled the door open to stand behind her, all five foot nothing of her ready for combat. 'It's true,' I said. 'You were shouting, Tommy. Some nursery rhyme ...'

The guards waited, patient. Tommy loomed in his doorframe, swollen belly protruding from under a stained vest. 'I've no idea what these two are talking about,' he said, measuring us with albino eyes. He stepped forward, wagged a finger at me. The smell of piss and stale sweat nearly made me gag. 'I could have you charged,' he said. 'For harassment.'

'Now Tommy, there's no need for that. These people were just concerned about you, that's all. I heard you myself from out in the street.' The Garda's voice, soft, cajoling. 'Listen, do you want me to call someone?'

'What for?' he said. Then, pausing. 'I could call a solicitor; this is an infringement on my rights. I know the law, you know. Don't think I don't.'

'Ah, I don't think there's any need for that, Tommy. So long as you're alright ... that's all anyone's concerned about.' The male guard this time. I'd say he'd taken one look at Tommy and was sorry he was the one got the call.

'And getting some sleep, that's what concerns me,' said Roz. 'Some of us have to get up in the morning.'

The male guard sighed. 'Right, well if there's no more trouble ...'

I pulled Roz inside the door and closed it, lest we were left facing Tommy while the other two belted it down the stairs.

I was no coward, but Tommy O'Keeffe was over six feet tall and could have been a rugby player in his day. The slack belly didn't take away from the strength in those shovel-like hands, and to find myself backed into a corner with him looming over me was, to say the least, the stuff of nightmares.

He'd been living next door for a while. Certainly, he'd been there before Roz moved in two years before, and in so far as we could, we both avoided him. We exchanged looks when we heard him coming up the stairs with his shopping, shouting in frustration if something happened to tumble from one of his bags and onto the floor, while he fumbled his key in the space between his apartment and ours.

Most of his time he spent outside in the complex car park. He marched up and down in a hi-visibility vest with nothing underneath, threatening any of the day trippers brave or stupid enough to try to get free parking when the seafront was jammed. Personally, I'd have circled the area ten times rather than have his red face roaring into mine. Sometimes, he'd sit sentry on the wall outside, eating a sandwich or a 99 from one of the kiosks over the street; it dripping down his front as he watched and waited – a troll blocking the main entrance to the building.

Roz had had a number of run-ins with him. There was the time he'd left his mountain bike in the small hallway between our two doors. Attached to the bicycle were two pannier bags, and the smell was as if something lay dead inside them. Roz, with a pair of marigolds on, had shunted the bike so that it barricaded his doorway, and had then taken a bottle of Febreeze and saturated the air with it to make her point. Another time, and although we hadn't seen him firsthand, we knew that he was the one responsible for the blood stains on the handle of the main door downstairs. Blood was smeared too on the glass where he'd placed his palm when opening it. Enraged, Roz had stomped into the apartment and typed up a sign: *Whoever is responsible for these bloodstains, you are vile. Disgusting!* That night we saw him peering at the glass – a rag of some kind in his hand. Proof of our assumption.

I thought Roz was going to lose her reason when we were awakened the following night with the same nursery rhyme belting through the wall. *Ding-Dong Johnny, Johnny ...* It began the same as the previous night – a chant that became a roar.

'That's it, they're going to have to do something ... this is fucking ridiculous,' Roz said, climbing over me and out of the bed to get to the phone. This time they took longer to come around. We'd been through fifty renditions of the dreaded rhyme and there was still no sign of them. Roz had gone into the spare room and begun hammering at the wall. 'Shut the fuck up,' she yelled. 'Shut. The. Fuck. Up.'

The management committee of the complex had said they'd have a chat with him, which we knew was as good as useless. No one else had complained. They were clearly, as Roz had put it, either deaf or terrified. The guards, when they finally showed, could do nothing either. Tommy, who had shut up as soon as they'd pulled into the car park, refused to answer the door. 'We could arrest him,' a guard told us when we'd been driven to going around to the station. 'But he'd be back home in an hour, and it wouldn't change a thing.'

'But what about mentally?' Roz asked him, 'Couldn't he be sectioned or something, for his own good? The man is clearly off his rocker.'

The guard sat back in his chair and studied us. 'It'd be the same thing. I could bring him in, get a psychiatrist to see him. Most likely he'd sweet talk the psych and he'd be back home that evening.'

'But the noise? I mean there has to be some law about the noise, surely?'

The guard sighed. 'That'd be very hard to prove. He'd have to be recorded, the ratio of decibels. I wouldn't bother if I were you. Best thing you can hope for is he stops. What about family? Is there anyone going in and out? Someone who might convince him to see a doctor?'

We shook our heads. No one darkened the door of number ten.

Roz and I hadn't particularly paid attention to the absence of the post. I'd been expecting a journal I subscribed to which hadn't turned up. Apart from that, we weren't exactly seeking bills in our mailbox. It wasn't until Roz came home one day and called me, her voice shaking, that we realised what had been going on.

Roz had got home before me, and as she was climbing the stairs she'd noticed something outside our door. She figured one of the neighbours had taken in a package for us; they often did. On closer inspection it was a filthy toilet roll package smeared with faeces on the outside, and inside were letters addressed to both of us, including my arts journal which had been ripped into smithereens.

Disgusted, she'd dropped the package, kicked it inside our door and gone into the apartment as quickly as she could and phoned me. 'Talk about an indirect threat,' she hissed down the phone. 'He's got it in for us now. God knows what he's going to do.'

'Is he there now?' I said. 'Was there any sound of him?'

'I don't know. The door was closed. What time will you get home?'

'God, I don't know. It's going to be late. There's a call I have to take from the States. We can't go anywhere till it comes. It'll be nine at the earliest. Will you be ok? Maybe you should go to your mother's?'

'No, I'll be alright. What's he going to do, kick the door in?'

Roz took the mail in its filthy bag round to the station. She didn't admit to it but I figured she'd broken down. Her eyes were still swollen when I got home. She was also livid. 'How fucking dare he?' she said. 'I swear, he'll pay for this.'

The Garda on duty, Roz told me, had known all about number ten. There'd been an incident a year ago which we'd heard nothing about – we were on honeymoon. Tommy had left a bath running and flooded the girl who was living in the flat below – thousands of euro worth of damage. She'd complained to the management committee. Of course, Tommy hadn't a bean to pay for it. After a liaison meeting to try to sort it out, Tommy had gone downstairs to accost the girl. He'd started banging on the door, and when she didn't answer, he'd begun kicking it. The girl, who'd been in there with her pregnant sister, was terrified. It was when he'd gone around to the front window and started banging on the glass that they'd called the guards.

'Why didn't they tell us that before?' I said. 'Why didn't that little weed O'Mahony say something?'

Roz shook her head. 'Probably something to do with privacy, I suppose. Still, Neil didn't have any problem telling me.'

'Neil?' I said.

'The Garda on duty.' She smiled. 'He said he'd have no problem coming around here and telling Tommy he'd kick the shit out of him. Fairly brave, don't you think?' she said.

I felt a stab of jealousy, took in her tousled state, and red eyes.

'I'll bet he did,' I said.

Roz smirked, giving me a look that said she was enjoying winding me up.

That night was quiet. 'Thanks be to Jesus,' I thought. Maybe whatever kind of breakdown he'd been having had passed. Probably drinking on top of the medication, Roz said. We couldn't be sure, but it was likely he was on some type of medication. And there was no doubting the reek of booze off him.

The next day I was up north at a meeting. The company was closing a deal on the sale of land for a wind farm. So many zeros in the contract it'd make your head spin. Afterwards the boss took us out for a meal to celebrate. We were onto the coffee stage when I noticed I had a missed call from Roz. 'Ring me,' she said. 'Soon as you get this.' I excused myself from the table and went outside.

'Christ, where have you been?' she said. 'He's been knocking at the door. Now, he's sitting on the wall outside, waiting to catch one of us going out.'

'You didn't answer?'

'Of course I didn't answer. It's one thing mouthing off at him in public ... wait, maybe that's what I should do. Go out while he's still down there. He can't do anything in a public place.'

'Is there anyone else in the building?'

A pause. 'Who knows? I see Nigel's car's there ... doesn't mean he's in, of course. Still, there'll be people passing ... better than having him outside the door and me trapped in here.'

My mind was swirling. But Roz was right, wasn't she? He couldn't try anything, not in public. Maybe he was even going to apologise. You never knew with Tommy O'Keeffe. 'Right, tell you what, go down. See if says something, but keep me on the phone ... I'll be there listening.'

'Great, you'll hear me getting throttled,' she joked. 'It'll be like that dude got eaten by the grizzly bear with his girlfriend recording the footage.'

'Roz!'

'Yeah?'

'Don't go provoking him,' I said. Everything went muffled then as she placed the phone in her pocket.

I could hear Roz go down the stairs, the click as she opened the front door, and another as she pulled it behind her. She'd have been behind him now, standing in the porch; three more steps and they were even. I counted six, and then she stopped and turned. He hadn't said anything.

'Tommy, don't suppose you saw anyone around our place yesterday, did you?'

An elongated silence.

Steps, three maybe, then a blip as Roz unlocked the car.

'Is that a question now, or an accusation?' The vowels drawn out. Smart arse counter-question.

'A question,' Roz answered. 'It's just someone tore up our mail and left it outside the door. The guards have it now, are fingerprinting it. I take it you didn't see anyone?'

In fairness she'd kept her tone even. Tommy O'Keeffe didn't answer. But she must have been three steps from the car when he spoke again.

'You come back here,' he said. 'It's my turn to ask you a question. A philosophical question, we'll say ...'

Shuffling, a few steps more. Was she walking away or towards him? Suddenly, his voice was louder, and I knew.

'Where's John?'

'At work, why?'

His voice low, so that I had to strain at the earpiece. 'How long does he want to live?'

Had I heard right? Roz gave a chuckle, a nervous one. 'What? Is that a threat, Tommy?'

The voice raised this time, so that there was no doubt. 'You ask John how long he wants to live. Me? I could die any time, I don't care. Question is ... how long do *you* want to live?'

Hurried steps. I prayed to God she was going towards the car. Prayed he wouldn't follow her, block her way as she tried to drive out of the car park.

'You're sick, you know that. You're a sick fuck.'

The car door slammed, I heard the engine start and the screech of the tyres as she drove away. It was a few minutes before she took the phone from her pocket and knocked it onto speaker.

'Did you hear that? Did you fucking hear that?'

'Every word. Christ. What now? You can't go back there.'

'I'm going around to the station. That's a threat, John. A bloody death threat! They can't let this go. We can't even live in our own home in peace. He's capable of it, you know. You should have seen the way he looked at me.

That fucking red face, just staring, stony like ... I really thought he'd be mad enough to try ...'

Garda Neil had taken it very seriously, Roz told me, when I collected her that night from her mother's. So seriously that he'd given her his mobile number in case she should need to contact him. He said the next time Tommy kicked off, they'd make sure to bring him in. They wouldn't be able to keep him – but he would be able to summon him to an urgent court appearance and try to obtain an ASBO. As soon as he broke that, which no doubt he would, we'd be home and dry. Tommy wouldn't be allowed within thirty feet of us, which meant he'd have to move out of number ten. In the meantime, Neil had said, it might be an idea not to go back there.

Roz and I crept up the stairs that night. The plan was to get some clothes, and whatever else we needed to get us through the next who knew how many days until they managed to pin him down and get him to court. In the meantime, we'd stay with her mother. All was quiet as I turned the key in the lock. Once inside, I pulled across the flimsy chain, and Roz laughed. 'You don't think that'd keep anyone out?' she said. We raced around the apartment, throwing things into our backpacks. Roz lingered at the bookshelf, wondering what she'd take to read. 'Come on,' I told her. 'The quicker we get out of here, the ...'

My words deadened by the sound of the knocker.

'Fuck,' Roz mouthed. 'I'll ring Neil.'

I stood dead centre of the living room, bag in my hand. 'Maybe it's not him. Could be one of the neighbours.'

Roz raised an eyebrow; she wasn't taking any chances. She crept into the bedroom with her phone.

The knocker went again as she came out of the bedroom. 'He's not answering,' she whispered. Why would he? I thought. Probably at home with his wife, his kids. And why should Roz have to go ringing another man anyway. 'Fuck it,' I said, 'I'm not putting up with this anymore.' I pulled open the door and there he was looming over us. 'Do you think you can fuckin' drive me out of here?' he said. His face was puce, waft of whiskey on his breath. He was wearing trousers, nothing else. 'We don't want any trouble, Tommy,' I said. He advanced, driving me back into the hall. 'Let's talk,' I said, 'Like civilised ...'

I don't know if he tripped or he pounced, but I fell backwards with the full weight of Tommy O'Keeffe on top of me. I heard Roz scream. She dropped her phone as she leapt on his back, but it didn't stop those shovel-like hands closing round my throat. I tried to manoeuvre myself out of his grip, but it was impossible. Spittle fell on my face as he roared like an animal. His words lost in my terror.

He must have turned when he felt the blow, one hand came off my neck, the big head swayed slightly to the side and she struck again. This time knocking him clear off me. I staggered to my feet. 'Roz, fuck ...' She was shaking, about to go at him again. 'Leave it,' I said. It was plain he was in no state to do anything. 'I'll call an ambulance.' She looked at the instrument in her hand. An iron sculpture that weighed a ton. 'Don't,' she said, both of us on our knees as the blood began to seep into our carpet. The phone began to ring; it rang and rang under the table where it had fallen. Neil's name flashing on the screen, but neither of us answered.

DEATH'S CHILD

'Bernard, stay still. Don't worry about what's over my shoulder.' Treasa, the social club coordinator, leaned in, her red lips and white face no more than an inch from his as she pencilled a black line round his eyes and then smudged it with her fingertips. Her nails glinted metallic silver. 'Such long lashes,' she said, fingering them as he blinked, 'any girl would die for those.' She straightened, and Bernie allowed his eyes to refocus. Treasa stood before him, long legs covered only by a man's white t-shirt, a red sticky substance running down its front. Her dark hair was back-combed, riotous. She kept brushing it back from her huge blue eyes. 'Shame you didn't dress up,' she said. 'You'd have made a mean Vampire Lestat.' She dipped her finger in the red paint and trailed a sliver of blood down his right cheek.

There was more excitement among the staff than the students, Bernie reckoned. The staffroom had become home to zombies, and several sexy witches who milled round in tight black dresses sporting pointy hats or devil horns. If they strolled through Temple Bar they could almost be mistaken for a hen party. 'Treasa, what are you supposed to be?' one of the witches shouted across the room. Treasa shrugged. 'Death's Child,' she said. 'More creative than a trying-to-be-sexy witch anyway,' she mumbled, giving Bernie a wink. 'Right, you're done Bern,' she said. 'Who's next?'

In the bar, Bernie was almost sorry he hadn't worn a costume; he felt more obvious because he looked normal. Normal was the kind of thing to attract attention on a night like this. The room was thronging with students. He saw Alvaro from Madrid flirting with Cynthia from Sao Paolo who was wearing – if wearing was not too strong a verb – a Wonder Woman costume that left little to wonder about.

The teachers, all bar Seanie who was mingling with the students, were clustered in a corner of the room. Bernie tuned in and out of the conversation and watched Seanie laughing with a girl in a Little Red Riding Hood costume. As though they sensed his eyes on them, they both suddenly turned. Seanie raised his beer glass to Bernie and gestured for him to join them. Embarrassed, Bernie saw no alternative and made his way through the tightly woven group between him and his friend.

Seanie. You'd think he'd have learned his lesson after the last time, but no – the students were adults, as he put it, and that meant fair game. Bernie liked Seanie, but sometimes he couldn't believe the nerve of the man. He'd marched into the director's office and asked her to move a student from his class after he'd had a one night thing with her. He'd been a gentleman, he'd said, even dropped her back into the city centre the next morning, but the girl had expected more – a relationship maybe. She'd started undermining him in class, making pointed comments. He figured she'd told some of the other students too. He'd had to tell the DOS what happened, and the girl had been moved, without so much as a reprimand for Seanie, to another class.

'Teacher!' Bernie was waylaid by a hand on his arm on his way to the men's. He turned to see Alessandro and Victor. The two boys were never apart. Neither had shown up for class that week. 'Where have you two been?' Bernie asked them. Victor laughed. 'Sorry teacher. We had parties all weekend.'

'Weekend?' Bernie said. 'But this is Wednesday!'

'It was a long weekend,' Victor grinned.

Alessandro nudged Bernie. 'What you think of the Brazilian girls, teacher. Hot, yeah?' He mimicked a burning movement with his hand and laughed.

Bernie laughed in turn, but didn't comment. He saw Seanie and Little Red Riding Hood disappear, probably gone out for a smoke. He exchanged a bit of banter with the two boys before disengaging himself and headed for the toilet.

He was climbing the stairs when he heard a sound, a laugh. Feet silent on the thick red carpet, Bernie stopped at the turn of the stairs to listen, then stole quietly towards the sound. A door was open just off the corridor. He noticed that there was no handle on the outside. He pushed the door open a couple of inches. It was a storeroom of some kind, and enough light shone from the streetlight outside for Bernie to make out two figures standing opposite the window. Seanie? A flash of white, a moan, the jingle of steel as a belt was undone. No! Bernie stepped back. A foreign voice whispering 'baby' as the hands crept beneath Death's Child's t-shirt. Bernie made her out in the orange haze – hair askew, bare legs wrapped round the waist of a cowboy as he slammed her hard against the wall.

'Christ,' Bernie thought. Treasa. And her with a long-term boyfriend. A nice guy, who normally showed up at the staff nights out. Damien, was that his name? He'd seen him tagged in Treasa's Facebook pictures. What the hell was the girl thinking? Silently, Bernie withdrew. He went into the men's and locked himself in a cubicle, ashamed that the sight of Treasa had got him aroused. Pretty, quirky Treasa. He'd have tried it himself if he'd thought he'd stood a chance. But not when she had a boyfriend; there were lines you just didn't cross. Anger surfaced as he remembered what a fool Deirdre had made of him. Six months it had been going on; she'd looked him full in the face and admitted it, no more remorse than a sociopath. She'd got bored, she said. Bored, that was a laugh and she the one who sat at home day after day watching mindless Netflix series. He didn't think she'd the energy to actually cheat on him.

Bernie cast a look at the door of the storeroom before hurrying down the stairs. He didn't hear anything. He practically collided with the school director as he pushed open the door to the bar. 'Bernie!' she said, 'She got you, too!' 'What?' The director waved her hand. 'Treasa, she did a great job on the faces.' Bernie didn't answer. He was taken aback for a moment by the director's outfit; a small black bowler was perched over her slick black bob. She'd glued fake lashes on one eye and a set of braces covered her man's white shirt. 'Barbara,' Bernie started. The eye was disconcerting. 'Not tonight, Bernie. Tonight, I'm Alex,' she said. Bernie tried to smile; he had one eye on the door waiting for Treasa and the cowboy to return. He leaned in towards the director. 'Maybe this is none of my business,' he said, 'but what if I were to tell you I'd seen a member of staff with a student upstairs? I know there's no rule against it, per se, but ...' Barbara moved closer. He smelt wine on her breath when she whispered 'where?' 'There's a storeroom. Turn right when you get to the top of the stairs.' Bernie went to get his coat. When he looked round the room, the director was gone. He stopped to talk to a couple of teachers on the way out, huddled outside the door smoking. 'Have you seen Seanie?' he asked them.

They shook their heads. He'd expected to find him sharing a cigarette with Little Red Riding Hood.

It was quiet in the staffroom the next morning. Two of the teachers had phoned in sick, and the director was hopping. Bernie glanced into the office on his way to class, but Treasa's desk was empty. He wondered if she'd rung in, too sick and ashamed to turn up for work, or if the director had got to her ... if she'd come upon her in the storeroom with her cowboy.

At break time, the director stuck her head out of the office and called him. He went in, heart skipping, wondering if she were about to tell him what had happened with Treasa. 'Bernie, is there any chance you could cover a class this afternoon?' she asked. Bernie considered for a minute. 'Yeah, sure. What level is it?' 'Upper-int. You should find the notes in Sean's folder.' Barbara didn't look up, and Bernie left the office feeling almost dissed. She was in some mood today. It seemed the staff weren't the only ones hungover.

'Where's Sean?' one of the students asked. 'I don't know,' Bernie said, 'sick, I think.' The blonde girl who Bernie recognised as Little Red Riding Hood looked concerned. He wondered if she'd spent the night with him.

Bernie was surprised when he finished class to see Seanie in the director's office. He moved around the staff room, pretending not to look, but everyone could see through the plate glass that separated the office from the staff room. The director was sitting erect in her leather chair, Seanie slumped somewhat in front of her. Bernie saw him spread his hands in a *what can I say?* gesture. The director stood, and Seanie did too. He didn't look happy. Bernie looked down at his papers as the door opened. He felt Seanie stop and pick up his coat from a chair nearby. He looked up. 'Seanie, I took your class this afternoon. I've written it up for you.' Bernie waved the folder at Seanie. The director came out of her office, walking quickly, head down. She looked upset. Seanie looked after her. 'Don't worry about it, Bern,' he said. He pulled on his leather jacket. 'Be seeing you.' A few people looked up and mumbled goodbye.

Friday came and Seanie hadn't returned. Bernie bumped into Treasa at the photocopier. She smiled at him – her red-coated smile. Her bracelets jingled as she worked the machine. 'How's Damien these days?' Bernie asked her. The smile left Treasa's face. 'Ah, I couldn't tell you, Bern. We're not together anymore.' 'Oh God, I'm sorry.' Bernie touched her braceleted arm. 'It's ok, we split up about three months ago.' 'Ah, ok. Sure, maybe we could get a coffee sometime. If you want to talk or anything.' He hoped it sounded casual. Treasa smiled. 'Yeah, maybe,' she said. She glanced round the room and then leaned in conspiratorially. 'Have you heard about Seanie?' she said. Bernie shook his head. 'He's not coming back. Apparently, the director walked in on him the other night with a student.' Bernie made a surprised sound. 'Not against the rules though, is it?' he said. Treasa raised an arched eyebrow and gathered her papers. 'Not yet, but they'll get you on something else. Think from here on in we'll all have to be careful.'

His eyes followed the sway of Treasa's hips as she climbed the stairs. Poor Seanie. He'd wondered where he'd vanished to with Little Red Riding Hood.

ASHES

The tent had been there for some time. But covered as it was with thick branches of coniferous trees no one had seen it. Or had at least failed to pay attention. It was Elsie, or more precisely Elsie's little dog, that found it while nosing around in the long grass for a ball.

Elsie was seventeen that summer. The days were long with her father out at work, and she complained that she had nothing to do. One day, she'd been on Facebook and she'd seen an ad – a dog rescue charity looking for a home for a small brown terrier. She'd shown it to her father who was doubtful at first. Elsie wasn't the sort of child trusted to take care of an animal, but then she wasn't a child anymore. This was a fact Elsie's father had to face up to. Despite her simplicity Elsie was becoming a young woman. He looked at her that day, at the long denim-clad legs stretched out on the couch, the shapely breasts under her childish yellow t-shirt. Maybe an animal would be good for her, teach her some responsibility. It would get her out of the house. But he warned her never to go too far. It was the dog that lured her to the woodlands.

Elsie had taken the path that led around the coast, but she'd veered off and up to the fields that led to the woods and eventually to the head with its cross on top. Up there the people looked like ants from the beach below. The Met Office had reported that it was the hottest summer in thirty years. It hadn't rained in weeks and the grass was beginning to yellow. As soon as they'd climbed the steps and got out into the open grass, she'd taken the lead off the small brown terrier who she'd named Biscuit. The dog had run on ahead, but not so far that he'd lose sight of his owner. He stopped every now and then for Elsie to catch up.

That morning, Elsie had taken Biscuit to the pet store. Her father had given her money, and she'd bought a plastic thrower with a rubber ball and a woolly sheep with a squeaker inside that the dog had torn open in minutes. The ball she'd kept inside her jacket until their trip to the fields. Now, with Biscuit off his lead, Elsie threw the ball. She brought her arm back in an arc, jumped and flung as far as she could, and the dog went bouncing after it. They continued like this until they'd reached the edge where the field met the woodland.

'Biscuit, come on boy!' Elsie yelled. She could see the dog nosing round in the grass, seemingly unable to find the rubber ball. 'Biscuit!' she shouted again, but the dog didn't come. She made her way through the long grass to where he was standing, nose going and tail straight, staring towards the circle of conifer branches, which Elsie could now see were hiding a brown tent. Its door was open and outside in the grass there was a girl reading.

'Hello.' The girl looked up from her book, stood up and stretched. 'That your dog?'

'Yes,' Elsie said.

'Cute little thing,' the girl said, kneeling and clicking her fingers to coax the dog, who stayed back, wary. 'Afraid he may have eaten some sardines I threw there, hope it doesn't sicken him.'

'Are you camping?' Elsie asked. She'd done that once with her parents. She remembered her father building a swing in the trees and her mother complaining about getting eaten by midges.

'No, we're living here. For now anyway,' the girl said. She put her hand down, cracked open a can of Coke. 'You want one?' she asked.

'Sure,' Elsie said. The dog had got braver now, and was sniffing around the camp at a purse containing cosmetics. Elsie had noticed that the girl was wearing makeup, which seemed strange living outdoors and everything. And she was younger than Elsie. She looked like a little girl playing grownups.

'You're pretty,' the girl said. Elsie smiled. Maybe she could be friends with this girl. She didn't have many friends. The kids at school thought she was strange. She knew she wasn't as clever as them, had to take special classes. Some of the boys liked her. At least she thought they did. One of them had stopped her one day in the corridor when her teacher had sent her on an errand. He'd pushed her hair back from her face, and he'd kissed her. But it wasn't like she thought a kiss would be. He'd pushed his tongue inside her mouth; it was strange, sloppy. Then he'd let her go, and she'd gone back to class with the taste of that boy in her mouth. A liquorice taste like he'd been eating blackjacks.

'Do you like reading?' the girl asked.

Elsie shook her head.

'You should, you know. You can learn a hell of a lot from reading.' The girl picked up the book to show her. On the cover there was a picture of a bare-chested man and a woman in a flimsy dress coming off her shoulders. Elsie had seen some of the girls at school swapping books like this. But they didn't keep them in the school library.

'Why are you living out here?' Elsie asked.

The girl shrugged. 'We had nowhere else to go. Besides, it's nice you know, the freedom.'

Elsie nodded. It did seem nice. From the fields you could see all the way down to the bay. She guessed at night the girl lit a campfire. Maybe she cooked beans and toast, the way her father had all those years ago. Toast was always better on a campfire. It tasted woody, like the outdoors itself.

'Who are you living here with?' Elsie asked, pushing the hair out of her face and taking a swig of the Coke.

'My boyfriend. We wanted to be together so we came out here where no one could bother us.'

'Where is he now?'

'Here he is.' The girl stood and waved. Elsie looked up, shaded her eyes against the sun. The dog started barking. A boy was coming across the field, bags in both hands. 'He went to get supplies,' the girl said. 'Hey, did you get everything?'

The boy nodded at Elsie. 'Who's this?' he said.

'I don't know,' the girl laughed. 'What's your name?'

Elsie was struggling with the dog. She'd put his lead on, but he was kicking up a racket. 'Elsie,' she said. 'And you?'

'Tessa and this ...'

'Shut up,' the boy said, abruptly. He dropped the shopping bags and flopped down in the grass.

'Why, she's just ...'

'Don't go telling people who we are,' the boy said.

The girl shrugged. 'Whatever. She's just walking her dog. She doesn't care about us.'

'I'd better go,' Elsie said.

The boy looked at her. 'You don't have to,' he said. The girl smiled. 'Yeah, stay,' she said. 'We could have something stronger than this.' She waved the can of Coke, searched in the boy's shopping bags and brought out something else. 'Oh, cider. You do like cider?' she said.

'No, really I'll have to go,' Elsie told them. 'But thanks for the Coke.'

The girl smiled. 'See you next time,' she said. And Elsie felt their eyes on her as she turned and walked back down the field with the dog.

That evening at dinner Elsie answered her father when he asked about her walk. But she didn't tell him about the couple she'd met, or the fact that she'd gone into the fields up by the woods. But she thought about them as she sat on the couch and watched TV that evening, while her father spent a very long time on the phone. She thought about the girl and how friendly she'd been, not like the girls she knew. She thought about the black lines around her eyes and how they made them look enormous. Elsie had never worn makeup. Her father didn't approve. Come to think of it, her mother hadn't either. At least she didn't think so. Her mother's face was beginning to fade. People said she looked just like her though, so she guessed she couldn't ever forget really. And that was good. Sometimes she talked to her in the mirror and imagined her answering back.

The boy had been funny. She thought about how he didn't want to tell her his name. He wasn't unfriendly though; he was ok. Not like the girl, but then boys were funny. You never knew what way to take them.

The next afternoon Elsie hooked Biscuit up to his lead and retraced her path from the previous day. This time she walked right up to the tent. The door was open, but there wasn't anybody there. Elsie looked around, saw a charcoal circle in the grass where the couple had lit a fire. The dog got a bit of burnt stick in his mouth and began to chaw on it.

'Hey, what are you doing here?' The girl had come up behind her from the woods. Her hair was wet and it hung sopping over one eye.

Elsie smiled. 'Just out walking,' she said. 'Thought I'd stop by.'

'Good,' the girl said. 'That's nice. You take him out every day?' She pointed to the dog, too busy chewing to notice.

'He's a rescue,' Elsie told her. 'Me and my dad saved him. His name's Biscuit.'

'Cute,' the girl said.

Elsie looked around the small camp. 'Where's the boy?'

'Oh, he's working. Got a job with the fair for the summer. He's running the Waltzers. You know the ones that spin round and round and it feels like maybe your neck's going to snap with the gravity?'

Elsie nodded, though she wasn't sure she knew what the girl meant. It was nice just sitting with her.

'You mind if I do something with your hair?' the girl asked.

Elsie shrugged. All she ever had done to her hair was a trim. It fell down her back in long ripples of blonde. 'Ok,' she said. And the girl sat on a rock and told her to sit in close to her. Elsie sat on the ground between the girl's knees. She felt her fingers in her hair, surprisingly tender.

'I'm going to give you a French braid,' the girl told her, and she began separating Elsie's hair into strands and plaiting them. Elsie sat back and closed her eyes, the sun on her face. The dog chewed the stick, and all they could hear was the birds.

Elsie began to spend all her days with the girl. She'd get up late and have breakfast, then she'd take Biscuit and they'd walk across the fields to the camp. Sometimes, the girl asked her to bring things. Things she said the boy always forgot to get when he went to the supermarket.

'He never thinks to get what I need,' she complained. Elsie didn't see the boy there. She always left before he came back up from the fair on the seafront. She did see him one day when she and her father brought the dog to the beach.

They stopped at one of the kiosks for a 99 and there he was standing at the edge of one of the rides. Every so often he'd give a push to one of these big armchairs full of kids, and it would start to spin and the kids would scream in delight or terror. There was loud thumping music that made it seem like a disco.

'Can I try some of this makeup on you?' the girl asked Elsie one day.

'Oh, I don't know.' Elsie said. Nervous that she'd have to go home with it on and her father wouldn't like it.

'It's ok. We can take it off again if you don't like it. It's not like it's a tattoo or something,' the girl pleaded. 'Go on, I'll bet you'll look so pretty.'

'Alright,' Elsie conceded.

It was starting to rain that day and the girl told Elsie to come inside the tent. It was surprisingly big. She couldn't stand up in it, but there was plenty of room for sitting. She liked how the shadows of things outside showed inside. Branches reaching like long fingers along the canvas. She sat opposite the girl as she daubed foundation on her cheeks and then began to work it in with her fingers. Next, she put some eyeshadow on her lids. She told Elsie to close her eyes, and Elsie was aware of her breath on her face, and when she opened her eyes again the girl was right up close to her.

'You've got a pretty mouth,' she said. She took out a tube of lipstick and told Elsie to open her mouth, then to gently rub her lips together. She held up a mirror and Elsie hardly recognised herself. The girl had made her eyes dark like hers. Her lips were pale and shiny. She didn't look like a child playing dress-up, the way the girl did. She looked like an adult.

'You should wear makeup all the time,' the girl said. 'You're a real knockout. I'd better not let Petey see you. Oops.' She covered her mouth with her hand. 'Don't let on I told you his name, will you?'

Elsie laughed. 'No.'

'You know you make me feel kind of tingly ... down there.' The girl took Elsie's hand; she guided it under her short skirt and inside her panties, so that Elsie felt the warm wetness between her legs. Slick of it on her fingers.

'Oh,' Elsie said, and she tried to pull her hand away, but the girl held it there and rubbed it a little back and forth, so that Elsie's fingers were damp, and she felt kind of funny.

'Do you like that?' the girl asked. Her eyes were glassy. She took Elsie's other hand and sucked on one finger. 'Don't worry,' the girl said. 'It's ok.' She put a hand behind Elsie's head and pulled her towards her. She flicked her tongue inside Elsie's mouth, and it felt good.

'Don't worry. Petey won't be back for ages yet. Let's have a little fun.'

Elsie had never been with a girl before. Hadn't been with a boy either, apart from that liquorice kiss. When the girl pulled up her t-shirt and clamped her mouth onto Elsie's nipple she thought she might die, but in a good way. She pulled at the girl's sweater, eager. The girl didn't stop her.

For the whole of that week, Elsie got out of bed and went to the fields. She had to tie the dog's lead to one of the tent's stays so he wouldn't wander. Every afternoon the girls made love. Sometimes, they didn't bother to go inside. The girl said she liked to make love in the grass, although Elsie found it somewhat ticklish. They didn't need to worry about passersby unless they came right up to the camp, so well hidden were they by the hedge of conifers.

At the weekend Elsie was restless. Her father liked to spend Saturdays with her. He'd take her out for lunch and then go for a walk on the promenade. Sometimes he'd take her to see a film. She'd always liked the time she'd spent with her dad, but now she just wanted to be with the girl.

She was quiet that Saturday. The sun was shining, and the seafront was packed with day trippers. Her father had brought a blanket, and instead of going to a restaurant, they bought fish and chips and ate them in the grass. The fish was greasy, her fingers slick with it. When she licked them, she longed for the girl. That evening, when they were at the cinema, she got a text message. 'Come tonight!' it said. A knot of excitement formed in her stomach. She wasn't sure how she'd manage to get out. When they got home she thanked her father and said she was tired. She hugged him, something she rarely did, and her father patted her back awkwardly.

Elsie didn't think to take a torch. And it was bright enough until she veered off the coastal path and up into the fields. Even then, the moon was enough to guide her. She picked her way through the long grass. The night was warm and it was just as well because she'd slipped out past her father, who was dozing in front of the television, without so much as stopping for a jacket. As soon as she got in range she heard the tent zipper go up and the girl stuck her head out. There was no campfire, just the girl in the tent with a flashlight.

'Wasn't sure you'd come,' the girl said.

'Didn't you get my text?'

'Yeah, but I wasn't sure.' The girl put her arms around her, kissed her hard on the mouth.

'Where's the boy?' Elsie asked.

'He's going for a beer with some of the boys from the fair. Said he'd be back late, that he wouldn't wake me.' The girl smiled in the lamplight.

They undressed quickly. The girl took Elsie's breasts in her mouth, first one and then the other. Elsie felt that tingle that the girl had mentioned the first time they'd been together.

'Hey, why don't we go outside?' the girl said. 'I'd like to do it in the woods. I've never done it in the woods before.'

But Elsie didn't want to. It was dark amongst those trees, and underfoot it was prickly. She pictured them running naked in the woods, two feral children. For all the girl's insistence she stayed firm, and when she put her mouth on the girl she stopped insisting.

Elsie lay on her back, aware of nothing but the girl's hands and her mouth and the way her hair fell over Elsie's body. 'Now you,' the girl murmured. And Elsie wriggled from under her, pinned the girl's wrists above her head and let her breasts hover just above the girl's red lips, teasing. This girl had taught her things, things she'd read about between the pages of those paperbacks that the girls in school read. Things she had never even imagined. Now she wondered if this was what they were all doing; her schoolmates. A game that she had been excluded from. But she didn't care because she had this girl with her raven's hair and full lips.

Elsie didn't hear the tent door being lifted. When the girl gasped under her, pride swelled in her belly. She didn't see the boy standing behind her. He must have moved stealthy as a cat. When she felt his hands on her shoulders she went to turn, shocked from her dream-like state, but he hushed her, told the girls to continue. 'Go on,' he told the girl, and she slid her fingers inside Elsie, even as she tried to buck backwards to rid herself of the boy's weight. When he pushed himself inside, there was pain. Pain like she'd never felt before, like something inside her had torn. It must have lasted no longer than five minutes. Five minutes of the boy's weight on top of her, of him pumping inside her ripping her insides open. His hands pinning her wrists just as hers pinned the girl's, and the girl sobbing beneath.

'Elsie,' the girl whispered, when the boy had left the tent to take a piss. 'Elsie, I swear I didn't know.' The girl tried to touch her face, but Elsie pushed her hand away. She took her clothes and ran naked through the fields.

Elsie didn't stop running until she was almost at the road. There was no one behind her, and she stopped and dressed behind the low wall. When she crept into the house her father had gone to bed. She hushed the dog who gave a low growl but stopped as soon as he realised it was his mistress. Elsie crawled into bed fully clothed, pulled the duvet up around her. Despite the warmth of the night, she couldn't stop shivering.

The next day, Elsie stayed home. The dog looked at her, expectantly. 'Not today, Biscuit,' she told him. When the girl sent a text, she didn't answer. *I didn't know*, it said. And a few minutes later. *You won't tell anyone, will you?* The phone rang, but Elsie didn't answer, and the girl left no message.

On Saturday, Elsie went to the seafront with her father. It was hot, and the dog panted as they walked the promenade. It hadn't rained in weeks, and the grass had yellowed to straw. The fair was still going, and on the Waltzers Elsie saw the boy. When she saw him her blood felt hot, and a nerve kicked off in her head. He was laughing with a bunch of giggling girls as he gave their big chair a spin, and Elsie wanted to push him right in front of it. But she didn't, and she turned away before the boy saw her.

No one knew how the gorse fire started. Could have been some careless picnic makers having a summer barbecue, or someone dropped a cigarette on the cliff walk. But like its name it spread – wild and rapid along the head and the surrounding woodland. Helicopters were brought in to try to curb it. They lowered buckets into the sea, dropped tons of water, but nothing would stop the blaze. Homes were evacuated when the fire got too close. On the news, it was reported that a homeless couple were burnt in their tent – no one could understand how they couldn't get out, but the whole neighbourhood lamented the tragedy. People had seen them about – a young girl and a boy. There was nothing left of their remains, but bones smouldering.

Elsie and her father watched the helicopters from the beach. The dog barked at the sound of the blades. Elsie thought of the girl and her heart ached. It ached long after the fires had died, when nothing remained but ashes.

AFTER ADA

It had been going on for years, and he'd failed to notice. All those mornings Barry had rung the bell, and he'd gone out and exchanged pleasantries as he signed for the package, then came back in and propped it on the mantlepiece where she'd see it after she returned from one of her walks.

'Another one for herself,' Barry would say. And Maurice would scrawl his signature, barely noticing his wife's name on the package, never so much as glancing at the postmark or wondering what was inside.

Ada was always reading. He never asked her what. Never assumed that the packages he signed for were anything other than the books that she'd ordered online. Sometimes, if something she was particularly excited about arrived she'd show it to him – but he had no interest in books, and paid no attention to the cover or any other detail when she lay next to him in bed, propped up by an extra pillow, engrossed. Instead, he would turn his back and pull on the eye mask she'd bought him when he'd complained that the light stopped him from sleeping.

It was only after Ada that he discovered. The bell rang, and given how early the hour was he knew it could be no one other than Barry. 'It's for Ada,' Barry said. Trace of discomfort in his usual easy tone. He turned the alien package in his hands and nodded. 'She must have ordered it. Suppose I'll see a lot less of you now she's gone. Only bills you'll be bringing.' Maurice signed his name and went back inside.

He propped the package on the mantelpiece, went into the kitchen and made himself a cup of tea. He was used to being alone at this time of the morning. Ada usually took the dog for a walk and didn't get back before ten. Except last time she didn't get back at all. A man out walking his dogs had found her – and Misty, their golden retriever, barking, then whining, trying to nudge her awake. The man had called an ambulance, but he knew even before the paramedics had got there that she was dead. He'd called the number on the tag on Misty's collar, and the phone had buzzed and jingled on the kitchen table. That was how Maurice had found out. A stranger calling him from the woods to tell him his wife had been found unconscious.

Now Maurice drank his tea and stared at the package, willing the last month to disappear, to slip away as easily as his wife had. And then, with a curiosity he'd never had before, he drained the last of his tea and tore the packet open.

The fact that it was a book was no surprise. He read the title and the author, but he'd never heard of either. Turning it in his hands, he absently read the blurb and then opened the cover. On the title page in black felt pen he read: *For Ada – kindred spirit – I hope you like this one as much as you did the last. Love, Alex.*

Maurice stared at the inscription. Then picked up the package and held it close to see the postmark, but it was only stamped *Portlaoise* and that was where the sorting office was, so it told him nothing at all.

He walked out into the hall, the book in his hand, Misty at his heels, and paused before entering the room that for years had been his wife's study. Ada's books lined the walls; they'd grown so tall they almost reached the ceiling. They teetered dangerously, and he knew if he were to take one out, the whole pile might come crashing down. They were stacked on the floor too, heaped in untidy mounds, some of them spilling out like upset shopping bags.

On Ada's desk though, was a neat row of books; they fitted together like dominoes, no more than ten to a bunch. He pulled out his wife's chair and sat at her extraordinarily neat workspace. Her laptop was there, lid closed, whatever words she'd been working on trailing off, never to be edited. Ada spent hours at that desk, Misty prone on the floor next to her. She'd taken a sabbatical from her job in the library when the Arts Council awarded her a bursary to work on a collection of poetry. Maurice hadn't thought much about it until then. A hobby was how he'd viewed Ada's writing. And then he found himself a year later at a gathering in a bookshop on the quays in Dublin and a crowd of people he'd never met before saying how wonderful it was: his wife's debut poetry collection.

He cast his mind back to that day. Had there been an Alex there? Was he … she … (because it occurred to him now that Alex could just as well be a woman) at Ada's book launch? What was that woman's name, that publisher? Jenny, Jackie … something like that. In truth, he'd been too baffled by it all to remember much except that his wife seemed to have achieved some minor celebrity two months shy of her fiftieth birthday.

Minor. That's what she used to call him for a joke. When he'd told her he'd been named after his father, she'd laughed and said 'well, I guess that would make you

Maurice minor, wouldn't it?' And that's what she'd put on his library card just out of mischief when it had come time to replace it.

Maurice had never darkened the door of a library until a neighbour mentioned that you could borrow DVDs. Then he'd been in and out every other day, taking films up to the counter where Ada would stamp them and make some comment if it was something she'd already seen. They discovered they shared a love of noir movies, which resulted in animated chats, and the disgruntled shuffle of feet and clearing of throats if there happened to be a queue behind him. Eventually, he'd bitten the bullet, told her they were showing *The Maltese Falcon* as part of a noir series in the Lighthouse Cinema, and she'd smiled and said yes, she'd love to go with him.

After the launch Ada had begun to go out more. She went to readings and to the launches of her fellow poets. There seemed to be one every other week, sometimes more frequently. On the advice of her publisher, she'd set up accounts on Facebook, Instagram and Twitter, and she spent much of her time updating these pages and acquiring a posse of virtual friends that commented on each other's cats, and plants and god-knows-what-else. But this was, apparently, what you had to do to get noticed.

One afternoon he'd gone along to a café where Ada was one of three poets reading. He applauded when everyone else did, but he found it impossible to concentrate. In truth, Ada hadn't asked him to accompany her and she didn't mind when he hadn't suggested going again. She knew it wasn't his thing, that he'd rather be in his workshop sawing and drilling. And that was fine. They didn't need to share everything.

Maurice looked at the things on Ada's desk. A small reading lamp to the left, and a set of drawers to the right. On the drawers stood a framed photo of the two of them on honeymoon in Santorini. There were no other pictures, no other people to fill them. They had met in middle age; too late, Ada had said, for children, though she was only forty five, and there were plenty who didn't let that stop them. She'd never expressed any regret though, and neither had he, though he wouldn't have minded the company now – someone other than the dog to look after. They'd have been good parents, he thought, if only he'd met her sooner.

Maurice looked at the neatly arranged books on his wife's desk, leaned in, picked one up and opened it. *For Ada – this one made me laugh and cry and so much more ... yours always, Alex.* He opened book after book, spines creasing beneath his fingers. *For Ada ... with love; For Ada ... with huge admiration.* Each one was dated and dedicated in that same black felt pen; twenty-seven books in all, the oldest dating back to Christmas twelve years ago. Two books every year (birthdays and Christmases), three extra, the explanation scrawled across the title page: *Couldn't wait till December – when I read this, all I could think of was you.* Twelve years earlier – the year that Ada had won that prize for debut poets; when she'd been interviewed on that arts programme on RTÉ; when her book had gone on to a second print run and the publisher, delighted to have made a profit on poetry, had urged her to write more.

Now Maurice closed the book in his hands, looked round Ada's study and wondered about the things he didn't know about his wife.

Idly, he pulled open the top drawer of the set and lifted out what was inside: Ada's passport, bank statements, an old driver's licence with a picture of his wife long before they'd met, her publishing contract, invoices, two passport photos, concert tickets she'd kept as mementos, receipts long out of date, nothing beyond the mundane. He put everything back and repeated the process with the other drawers only to yield more of the same. And then he pulled open the drawer in her desk.

In this drawer he found several notebooks – he flicked through the pages, and mostly what he found there were fragments or drafts of poems. Ideas that may or may not have come to fruition before the end of her life. He kept looking. Finally, he lit on a notebook labelled *addresses* in his wife's clear hand. It was not an address book, just an ordinary lined reporter's notebook. He opened it up and saw the names and addresses of their friends, and then with nothing other to single it out than its strangeness – Alex Peyton – and an address in West Cork.

Maurice gathered up the books dedicated to his wife and brought them into the living room. Then he returned to the study for a writing pad and a pen from Ada's desk, sat himself down at the kitchen table and began to write the first letter he'd written in decades:

Dear Alex,

~~My name is Maurice Lynch. Ada died last month.~~

Too direct. And why the need to introduce himself? If this person was a friend of Ada's, as they clearly were, they would know about him, wouldn't they? She'd have spoken of her husband.

I'm writing to tell you the dreadful news that Ada has passed away.

Better. Gentler. It would help, he thought, if he knew who he was writing to – whether his tone should be brusquer or more refined.

Last month while out walking our dog, Misty, she took a heart attack and did not recover. It is strange writing to you as we've never met, ~~and I know nothing about the nature of your relationship to my wife.~~

Too accusatory. Did he really believe that Ada had been unfaithful to him? That she'd met some bookish type more in keeping with her own passions? Some foppish man with soft hands who'd never known a physical day's work, but sat by an open window dreaming up sonnets? The truth was he didn't know what to think. A part of him didn't want to think about it at all. He could bin the books, or better still burn them – but then they would keep coming, wouldn't they? He'd be forever dreading the post if he didn't tell this Alex that Ada was dead.

As Maurice sat at the kitchen table, writing then crossing out lines and re-wording them, Misty prone at his feet, he understood something of what it must have been like to be Ada – to feel as she felt as she sat at her desk day after day trying to get the words right.

Finally, satisfied with his letter, he read it out loud. His voice sounded strange, unpractised, in the empty room. His audience of one, Misty, perked up her ears and cocked her head to one side to listen:

Dear Alex,

I'm writing to tell you the dreadful news that Ada has passed away. Last month while out walking our dog, Misty, she took a heart attack and did not recover. We've never met and so I'm not sure how it was that you knew my wife, but given your long correspondence I know you will be sad to hear such news. I am returning the many books that you sent her – given their personal inscriptions, I would not like to pass them on to anyone else, and you may like to keep them. How is it that you knew Ada? Through the world of books, I suspect? I've never been much of a reader myself. No doubt she told you that. Anyway, nothing pains me more than to write this.

Sincerely,

Maurice Lynch

'That'll do, won't it girl?' he said, bending to ruffle the dog's ears. She pushed her head against his hand lovingly. She'd not been the same since Ada's passing. And he knew that animals grieved too, that they were in this together.

A week had passed since Maurice had posted the parcel of books to West Cork. He was sitting having his midmorning coffee when the doorbell rang, and he went out to find Barry standing there.

'Just thought I'd check in,' he said, handing him a scant few envelopes. 'See how you're getting on?'

'Ah you know, good days and bad,' Maurice said, eyeing an envelope addressed to him in black felt pen. 'It's quiet you know, after it all dies down. Everyone gets on with their own lives. And that's how it should be, I suppose ... you can't expect anyone to sit holding your hand.'

The envelope felt flimsy – no book this time, just a cursory note, one that would leave him with more questions than answers, or so he imagined.

'Would you like a mug of tea?' he said, desperate to postpone the moment when he'd have to open it – when he'd have to read what was unsaid beneath the platitudes.

'Ah, I'd best not,' Barry said. 'I've this lot to get through. Another time though? Maybe even make it a pint?'

He watched Barry cycle off – saw him get off the bike again further up the street before he turned and went back inside the house. Maurice looked at the other envelopes, knew what they were without even opening them: gas bill, bank statement, TV licence reminder. He gathered them all, took one more look at that now familiar hand, and threw them into the fireplace, struck a match and watched as the blue-yellow flame licked its way up the corner of one envelope until they all caught. There was no need to read what he already knew. No need to dwell on anything.

THE DRIVER

'You have to hand it to him,' Siobhan says, taking a sip of whatever newfangled blend of tea she's drinking.

'Hand it to him how?' I say.

'Well, putting himself through college like that. What was it you said he was doing?'

'Environmental biology.' I stand back to survey the bouquet, then reach for the scissors and the roll of tape on the countertop.

Siobhan readjusts her silk blouse on her narrow shoulders. 'It's not something I'd have expected ...'

'What? From someone like him you mean? Someone from that neighbourhood?' I grip the flowers tighter, winding the tape from base to stem.

'No, that's not what I meant ... I simply meant it's ... admirable.' Siobhan's hand makes an arc in the air like an actress in a Shakespearean drama. 'You know the father's not around?' she says, leaning one elbow on the counter. A smooth duck-egg pendant, too large not to be vulgar, swings onto her right breast and rests there. It lurches again, pendulum-like, as she shifts to examine my work.

'Would you say that if he'd been brought up in Foxrock?' I say, ignoring the comment about the boy's father.

She shrugs. 'Probably not. I don't mean anything derogatory by it, but where he's from, as you say, it wouldn't be the most ... aspirational area.'

'Oh, you're wrong there, Siobhan. We're all upwardly mobile now,' I say, fingers rapidly binding. 'Did you know we went to the same school? He even had my old maths teacher. Thought the old bugger'd be retired by now.'

That takes her aback. 'I didn't know you were from that side of town. You don't have an accent.' The pendulum swings again as she leans in. 'You'd have known his father then, wouldn't you?' she asks.

'I don't know. Maybe.' I twist to retrieve the scissors so she doesn't see the heat that creeps up my neck and sets my face aflame.

Siobhan was in Malta when Marty Moyes, who'd been working for the shop for a decade, had taken a heart attack. The doctors, his wife had said, expected him to make a full recovery, but it would be a while before they'd let him behind the wheel again. I'd phoned Siobhan, told her what was happening, and she'd given me the go-ahead to advertise for a new driver.

That day, as I attempted to do the deliveries on my lunch break, I stopped off at a newsagent's near UCD and asked if I could put an advert in their window. Students were always looking for jobs. And that was where Conor Delaney had seen it.

I'd just turned the sign to 'closed' and was sweeping cuttings into a pile when there was a rap of knuckles on glass. I looked up to see a young man eyeing me intently. 'We're closed,' I told him, pointing to the sign.

'There was an ad for a driver. Have you filled it?'

'No.' I unlocked the door and he passed, this fair-haired

giant, into the flower shop. I worried that he'd turn and, in doing so, smash all around him, but he stood patiently and waited. 'Do you have a full licence?' I asked.

He nodded, took a card from his wallet and held it out. His hands were huge. This young man had no place in a flower shop. He could crush everything in it – he could crush me. I took the card he offered, read the name in bold letters before my eyes slid down to the address beneath. An address I knew by heart. I handed the licence back to him, surprised as I did so that my hand remained steady. The trembling was on the inside. I could have turned him away then, told him I'd call him and never would, but something stopped me. 'Do you have any experience?' I asked.

He shook his head. 'I'm a student. I'll work hard.' He looked nothing like his father, but his voice, his timbre, was identical. There was some resemblance too in the fierce way he looked at me.

'Any penalty points?'

'No.'

'Well, we are pretty stuck. Is there any chance you could start tomorrow?'

He smiled and held out his giant's hand. 'I won't let you down.' His fingers closed round mine and I nodded, dumb.

He worked every day between nine and two. His classes were in the afternoons and in the evenings he'd come for the following day's list. He'd sit up at the counter and plan his route, checking Google Maps for locations and the easiest ways to get there. That first week I waited, convinced that Conor's turning up here was more than just coincidence, but as the days passed we grew easy with one another. I'd make tea and he'd tell me things. Not private things, but about his classes and funny incidents which seemed to happen daily. I wished that Siobhan would stay away and it could be just the two of us for another while.

'He's a bit young, isn't he?' Siobhan said, eyeing Conor as

he loaded up the back of the car.

I shrugged. 'If you compare him to poor Marty, I suppose he is. But he's careful, and he's got his full licence.' I didn't want to say it, but he also managed to get through the deliveries in half the time Marty Moyes did. That man was, after all, over seventy.

Siobhan watches Conor with undisguised interest. She asks him about his studies, and clearly she's asked him other questions too, to have gleaned that his father isn't in the picture. Siobhan's nosey like that. I've learned how to handle her over the years, found ways to deflect unwanted curiosity. I don't know what Conor's told her about his father, and I'm not about to ask. That would be to invite all kinds of unwanted questions.

I'd met Darragh Delaney in secondary school. He saved me from getting smacked in the face by a basketball – intercepted it as one of his classmates lobbed it across the corridor to bounce against the wall. I'd jumped back in fright and Darragh had smiled at me briefly as he knocked it clear, shouting *Hickey, you moron ... will you watch it?* After that he nodded to me in the corridor. Hickey teased me, pretending he was going to throw the basketball at me whenever I passed. He'd make as if to launch the ball, then let it slip through his hands before he bounced it and laughed.

The fifth years had art class directly before we had, and I discovered that Darragh Delaney usually sat in the same place I did. He realised it too because soon coded messages started to appear etched into the huge wooden table in the form of song lyrics. After each quote, the initial D appeared. Standing outside the art room, I watched Darragh pack up his bag. Some days he'd nod as he passed me on his way out, others he'd pretend not to have seen me. I started to etch responses to his lyrics. Usually I knew them, they ranged from Bon Jovi to Meatloaf, but if I didn't recognise the song I'd reply with something different. Anything to keep the thread going – and it did. For months it continued before anything actually happened.

My route home from school consisted of an uphill climb and a trek across a field before I exited through a gap in the railings. Darragh took this way home too, but he was usually with Hickey and some of the others, so I'd stay a good distance behind. One day, though, I was walking home and I noticed Darragh in front of me. There was a sixth year, who I knew to see, walking quickly behind him. When the boy got almost level with Darragh he pulled his backpack hard, knocking him to the ground, and proceeded to kick him. I looked around, panicked, but the closest bunch of students were far behind me, and by this time Darragh's assailant had walked away, leaving him pulling himself up from the ground, his school uniform covered in mud.

'Hey – are you alright?' I asked, breathless from the run to catch up with him.

'Yeah, fucking asshole,' he said. He was turning his glasses in his hands. One lens had been cracked and the left arm was hanging loose from the frame.

'Do you know him?'

'Yeah. Gareth Hynes,' he said.

'What happened? I mean why did he do that?'

Darragh folded his glasses and put them in his pocket. Without them I noticed that his eyes were an almost transparent green. 'He reckons an amp I've got was nicked from his garage.'

'Why does he think that?'

'Because, unfortunately for me, he's probably right, but I paid fifty quid for it and there's no way I can get my money back.'

'What'll you do?'

'Give him back his amp, I suppose, and suffer the loss.

He'll never let it go.'

'Why don't you tell him who you got it from?'

He looked at me as if I were totally naive. 'What? And risk an even worse thrashing? You must be joking.'

I blushed at my own stupidity and tried to think of something to say to redeem myself. We'd exited the gap in the railings, reached the point where I turned off left for home. We'd both slowed our step. 'How long have you been playing?' I asked.

'A few years. I'm a bassist.'

'Oh yeah?'

'Yeah. Lead is lead,' he said, 'but bass ... bass is the backbone of the band. Which way are you going?' he asked.

I pointed in the direction of home. 'Come on,' he said. 'I'll walk you.'

'Conor?'

He's sitting up at the counter staring at nothing. 'Sorry?' When he looks up, his eyes are huge, startled.

'Is everything alright? You've been miles away.' I put two mugs of tea on the counter and sit on the stool next to him. Siobhan is off today and it's just the two of us. Conor takes a Kimberly biscuit from the packet between us and chews distractedly. 'Is it a girl?' I tease. He shakes his head; then looks at me, that intent stare, like he's sussing me out, wondering if he can trust me.

'It's just family stuff,' he says then.

I nod, sip my tea. He tells me about some experiment they did in the university that went terribly wrong, resulted in the third years setting the lab on fire, but even as he tells the story, he's not really in it. Not like he normally is, and I'm pretty sure I know the reason.

When the poster went up outside the Martello bar, it had been more than a decade since I'd seen Darragh Delaney. We'd parted amicably – as amicably as you can at eighteen. He wanted to pursue his music career; didn't have time for a girlfriend. If you didn't make it by twenty five, he said, you never would; the industry wanted young people. I knew the real reason was my refusal to sleep with him.

Skinny Lizzy the poster read. I remembered how adamant he'd been that he'd never play in a tribute band. I examined the photo. He looked the same – was carrying a bit more weight round the face, but there was no doubting it was him. I thought I recognised one of the others too, but I wasn't sure. For whatever madness I decided to go to see them.

I didn't tell the friends I invited that I knew him. Instead, I feigned surprise when I ran into him at the bar before the gig. He was delighted to see me, asked if we could have a drink after. His friends had to call him several times for the sound check.

'Don't go anywhere,' he said, squeezing my shoulder, and I knew that I shouldn't have come.

Afterwards, I waited as he and the rest of the band loaded up the van.

'How come you're here tonight ... I mean you didn't ...?' Darragh waved his hand, a small smile on his lips.

'What? Come to see you?' I said. 'No. It's my local. They've always got bands ... they're usually good.'

'Lovely,' he said, lifting his glass. 'Cheers for that.'

I laughed. 'Anyway, whatever happened to your antipathy for cover outfits? Musicians cashing in on other people's talent, isn't that what you used to say?'

Darragh rounded his shoulders over his pint. 'Youth and optimism,' he said. 'They've both flown west. If you don't make it by twenty five ...' I knew the rest before he said it.

We stayed talking that night till closing time. He told me that he'd married at twenty two, so much for focusing on his music career. 'She was pregnant,' he said, 'with Conor. He's almost ten now.' When he walked me back to the flat, I didn't invite him in. We stood awkwardly until I flagged down a taxi for him, not wanting a long goodbye, but he still managed to pull me into a hug. As he held me against him, I thought of the rangy teenager he was. Now he was solid without being overweight. When he released me abruptly, I almost toppled over. 'It's been great,' he said. He hopped in the taxi and with a small wave vanished into the night.

We should have left it at that, but the next day I got a friend request on Facebook, and a month later a private message telling me that he was playing in Jim Doyle's if I was free. I wasn't, but I turned up anyway. I needed to exorcise him. Since the previous meeting he'd been living inside my head. It didn't work, of course, and that night he followed me up to the flat without being invited.

Conor continues to be distracted during the days that follow. He's not the only one. I began counting down months before, even though Darragh had cut all contact. On the Wednesday, two customers phone to complain about a serious mix-up; a funeral spray has been delivered to a wedding. Unfortunately, it's Siobhan who takes the call. 'This would never have happened with Marty,' she rages. Conor, luckily, is still out doing deliveries and I tell her that I'll deal with it.

He's devastated when I tell him. 'I'm sorry Lillian. Is Siobhan hopping? I suppose that's it now.'

'Look, it could happen to anyone,' I tell him. 'Human error.'

He shakes his head. 'No, it shouldn't have happened. It's my fault, I've been distracted. My old man's getting out of prison this week. I haven't seen him in eight years.' He digs into his jeans pocket and pulls out a folded piece of paper. 'He wrote to me, wants to meet ...'

I nod, eye the paper in his hand, wondering if he wants me to read it, but he doesn't offer, puts it back in his pocket instead. 'He killed a man,' he tells me. 'Got in a car drunk.'

We'd taken Darragh's car that night. The idea was that I would drive us home, but then he'd got the text from Anne-Marie telling him he couldn't take Conor out the following day, and he'd grabbed the keys and left the bar in a rage to confront her.

'Darragh,' I'd shouted, grabbing my coat and running to catch up.

'What?' he said, turning. 'She can't do this. I have rights.'

'Look, you can't drive, not like this,' I said, reaching for the keys.

He held them out of my reach. 'I'm fine,' he said.

'You're not.'

'Right, you drive me then.'

I shook my head. 'It's not a good idea. Wait till the morning ...'

'No, I'm going to sort this out. Come on. I'll drop you on the way.'

I refused to get in the car. 'Suit yourself,' he said. He'd jumped in then, slamming the door after him. He'd practically skidded out of the carpark. As he took the bend beneath the bridge he mounted the curb, didn't even see the elderly man until he'd felt the thump.

'Do you want to see him?' I ask.

Conor hangs his head. 'I don't know.'

'He is your dad.'

'Yeah, I'm thinking about it.' He drains his tea. By the time he gets up to leave, he still looks unhappy.

'Hey, Conor,' I say.

'Yeah?'

'You put some hex on that wedding today.' We both begin to laugh. 'Not to mention the message of congratulations to the late Frank Devine.'

Days pass. Conor works hard. He doesn't say anything else about his father. When Darragh was sentenced he told me to forget about him. I visited him in prison, but he refused to see me. I wrote to him; he didn't reply. I needed to know if he resented me. If I hadn't turned up at his gig that night he might still have been with Anne-Marie. Even though he didn't acknowledge them, I sent him things – books mostly and an mp3 player with all his favourite music. I don't know if he was allowed keep it.

On Wednesday morning, Conor comes in from loading up the van. I'm busy working on a bridal bouquet. 'Lillian, do you think it would be ok to take Friday off?' he asks. 'Or to do the deliveries a bit later? I could come in the afternoon.' I stop what I'm doing, turn to look at him standing there, awkward. 'I wouldn't ask,' he says, 'but I'm collecting my dad.'

'Don't worry,' I tell him. 'Siobhan's here on Friday so I can do the deliveries.'

He smiles. 'Thanks,' he says. He takes a step towards me and for a moment I think he's about to give me a hug. I turn away from him, pick up the pruners, and fight the urge to tell him everything.

No Star Lesbian

I wouldn't have gone to the International Bar that night if Shirley hadn't cajoled me. Newly separated from Mike, she claimed to be enjoying single life. Yet, she was determined not to stay that way.

We had just collected several sacks of her stuff from the house they shared in Killiney – a beautiful four bed on the Vico Road three doors down from Bono's – and I'd strained a muscle in my lower back hauling yet another bag of Shirley's clothes from the car and into what, thankfully, was a ground-floor apartment in a complex overlooking Fairview Park.

'Bit of a step down in the world,' I said, as Shirley gave me the not-so-grand tour of her new quarters, which consisted of a living room, tiny kitchenette, shower room and a surprisingly decent-sized bedroom with a double bed.

'You can't put a price on freedom,' she said, flopping down on the bare mattress, patting the space beside her, 'and besides just think of all the action this baby's going to see.'

Despite myself, I laughed. Shirley had always been insatiable.

In the early days of their relationship, she had regaled us with stories of her and Mike's sexual exploits. Mike was younger than Shirley and that apparently made all the difference. Shirley's previous paramour, a government minister, hadn't been able to keep up with these feats of gymnastics and so she'd moved on, no compassion and no regrets. When he appeared, as he often did, on television, I could never get out of my head Shirley's stories about the poor man's shortcomings.

'Right,' she said, jumping up to rummage in a bin liner from which she pulled a sparkly top, 'how about we go into town and have a drink to celebrate?'

I looked at my watch. 'What about this lot?' I said.

She shrugged. 'It's not going anywhere. It's mostly just clothes. As far as I'm concerned, he can keep everything else. Come on – there's a gig I'd like to catch in the International – it's been ages since we hit the town. Humour me?'

Dublin was alive no matter the night. We crossed the Liffey, sidestepped the gangs of foreign students that tramped the cobbled streets of Temple Bar, and made our way across to Wicklow Street.

Outside the International Bar a few people stood around smoking. A woman with her hair shaved on one side, and quiffed and dyed blue on the other, stepped out of our way as we entered. A poster inside the doors advertised a comedy night upstairs, while the gig Shirley had mentioned was due to start at eight in the basement. *Women Who Rock*, it was called – which didn't sound like the best place to pick up a man.

We were early and the place had yet to fill up. I got us a couple of seats at a table set back from the stage while Shirley went to the bar.

'Do you not get sick of it?' she asked me a few minutes later, as she sipped her gin and eyed up a young lad in tight black jeans and a black t-shirt who was setting up a mic on the small stage.

'What?' I said.

'Sitting at home watching Netflix with Arthur. The whole domestic bliss bullshit. Don't you ever want to just get up, walk out that door and never look back? Does he still even do it for you? You've always been cagey about that. What *is* Art like behind closed doors? He's holding his own, I'll have to hand it to him, but do you never see some young fella, and think yeah, I could do with a bit of that.'

I laughed as Shirley's eyes followed the lad in denims, at least twenty years her junior, who was now bending over to secure some cables, as the first musician, a fiery-haired girl in an oversized shirt, came on stage to do a sound check.

'Relationships change over time,' I said. 'It becomes more about companionship.'

Shirley snorted into her drink. 'That's exactly what I'm talking about. What happens to the razzamatazz, to the not being able to keep your hands off each other?'

The door opened and the blue-haired woman walked in with two other women; one squat and wearing glasses, while the other ballooned out of a checked shirt and bore an incredible likeness to John Goodman.

There was something about this group that stilled the statement I'd been about to make about not expecting to swing from the chandeliers at forty.

The fiery-haired girl was ready to start now. She'd been joined by a waif-like creature on violin and a somewhat sturdier bass player. Unfortunately, as it turned out, vocals were not this redhead's strong point and she whined her way through a set, which by the time they'd finished met with rapturous applause and a too-loud 'thank fuck' from Shirley, which sent me scurrying to the ladies.

When I came out the blue-haired woman was perched on a bar stool on the stage, a wrecked guitar that sported a crater-sized hole strapped across her chest as she banged out a test tune and called for more voltage. Shirley, who was already two gins ahead of me, was flirting with the barman.

'Right,' the blue-haired woman said, surveying the room. 'My name's Andy. As you can probably tell I'm not from around here. I'm second-generation Irish and grew up in Boston.' A few whoops went up from a gang that had congregated by the door. The woman smiled and began to belt out a song.

'Christ, she's good,' Shirley said, rocking in her chair and splashing me with her gin.

'So, this next song is about identity. It goes out to all those individuals who're only comfortable when plastering a label on a woman like me. It's called *No Star Lesbian.*'

A big cheer from the woman in the checked shirt. 'You tell 'em, Andy!'

Wolf whistles as the woman stood up from the bar stool and strutted to the front of the stage. She scanned the audience, wolf-like. With her high cheekbones and kohl-rimmed eyes, she was striking, but it was her self-assuredness that caught and held the attention of everyone in that basement.

'She's got real balls, doesn't she?' Shirley shouted above the clang of the guitar. I nodded, transfixed.

After the set, Andy climbed down from the stage to a volley of appreciation. The next act set up – a duo, one on keyboard, the other on vocals – two pale girls that could've been sisters. Andy joined the couple she'd come in with, took out a pouch of tobacco and began rolling herself a cigarette.

'Now aren't you glad you came out?' Shirley said, draining her glass and standing a tad unsteadily.

'Listen, Shirley, you wouldn't have a cigarette, would you?' I said.

'What? Since when are you back on the fags?'

'I have the occasional one. And like you said, it's been an age since I've been out.'

Shirley shrugged and rummaged in her bag. I'd already noted Andy pulling on a leather jacket and disappearing upstairs. Her guitar case still rested against the wall signifying her return.

She was being talked at by a bear of a man. He loomed in front of her, driven back only when she failed to turn her head, blinding him instead with her smoke. She looked away, bored, but still the man chuckled and gesticulated. She tapped her ash on his well-polished brogues, but he didn't appear to notice. I clutched the cigarette I'd bummed from Shirley and slipped the lighter into my pocket. A hazy rain blew in my face.

'I'm sorry, you wouldn't happen to have a light?'

She turned, glad, it seemed, of the distraction. But instead of offering me a lighter she proffered her cigarette and I leaned in, cupped my hands, and lit my cigarette from hers. The man, clearly disgruntled at losing his audience, moved on.

'So, what exactly *is* a No Star Lesbian?' I asked, coughing as the smoke hit my lungs. It must've been six years since I'd had one.

Andy laughed and blew smoke out the corner of her mouth. 'Well, you have to be familiar with the star system,' she told me. 'A gold star is a lesbian who's never slept with a man. Silver is a woman who's slept with a man once and it was enough to turn her; bronze just means your bi ...'

'So, No star is someone who refuses to be classified,' I said.

'Now you've got it,' she looked at me through hooded eyes and grinned.

'What about you? How long have you been married?' she asked.

'Who says I'm married?'

'You look married,' she said. 'And there's the ring. Unless you're trying to keep unwanteds at bay.'

I laughed, feeling stupid. 'Did you not see the queue? I had to come out here to escape.'

Just then her friend, the one who looked like John Goodman, appeared, squat girlfriend trailing behind. 'We're going to head off, Andy. School night and all.' Andy nodded, her face damp with rain, the perfect lines round her eyes smudging.

I looked at my watch. 'Better head back in,' I said, wondering what trouble Shirley might have got herself into in my absence.

Andy nodded, exhaled a cloud of smoke. 'What's your name anyway?' she called.

'Mia. Mia Jones.' Just then my phone blipped. *Sitting here like a bloody lemon*, it said. I turned and went back inside.

'Jesus, is this it?' Shirley groaned, waving her empty glass. 'Is this how it's going to be?'

I laughed. 'Think you may have chosen the wrong gig.'

'You're telling me,' she said. 'Closest thing to a man here was that big bird in the checked shirt. And even she was taken.'

'How's Shirley?' Art called. He was in bed when I got home, propped up against the pillows reading.

'Feeling a bit sorry for herself,' I said, toothbrush in one hand, mobile in the other. I had looked up Andy on Facebook and followed her page. Now the phone had pinged, and a small flag heralded a friend request as the toothpaste slid off my brush and into the hand basin.

'Louise rang,' he said. 'Said she'd be home at the weekend.'

'About time,' I answered, distracted. I turned on the tap and the blob of toothpaste swirled down the plughole. We hadn't seen our daughter for weeks. When Louise had chosen to enrol on an Arts degree at NUI Galway we'd been surprised. 'I'd like to get away, have the whole college experience,' she'd said. 'I'm not going to get that in Dublin.' At first, she'd been homesick, calling every couple of nights, taking the bus home every weekend. But after about six months that had stopped. Now we were lucky to see her every three weeks.

Louise wasn't the only one that had had to adjust. We'd had to adjust too. It had been eighteen years since we'd been alone together. In the beginning it was strange. We'd sit across from one another at the dinner table and the words wouldn't come. Louise's chatter had never allowed for silence, and so without her we'd sat somewhat bewildered in this new quieter world, until little by little we learned to embrace it.

I thumbed the friend request. Art said something I didn't catch. Andy O'Reilly. Picture of her standing in a graffitied doorway cradling a Persian cat. No blue hair; it wasn't shaved either. She was wearing leather trousers and a psychedelic top. As I swiped through her photos, I saw that it was one of several taken to promote an EP she'd made two years before. I tapped the screen and went back to her profile: Singer at freelance. Lives in Dublin.

From Boston, USA. My finger hovered. Accept. Decline. Accept.

The chats became a regular thing. Art joked that I was spending more time on social media than Louise. Not that we knew how much time Louise spent doing anything these days, except that a good part of her time was spent staring at her phone and grinning to herself when she did come home, which led me to suspect she'd met someone in Galway. All I hoped was that she was being careful. 'It's not like that, Mam,' she said, turning red, when I tried talking to her about it. 'We're mates, we hang out, that's all.' His name was David.

Louise had a point. There was nothing wrong with hanging out, was there? Nothing wrong with endless WhatsApp chats and Facebook messages. 'Jeez, does that thing ever stop?' Art said one night, as my phoned vibrated on the arm of the couch, and I shrugged and managed not to pick it up though I was itching to. 'Suppose Shirley has a lot of time on her hands,' he said then. 'Has she managed to pick up some young buck yet?' He laughed, and I felt disloyal to Shirley, thinking maybe I'd told him more than I should have.

I didn't tell him that Shirley had in fact picked up a young buck, as he put it. She'd met him at a salsa class in the Arlington Hotel, a Brazilian student who was here to study English. When she told me he was twenty six, I nearly choked on my latte. 'Jesus, your face,' Shirley said, squaring me in the lens of an imaginary camera. 'It's just a bit of fun, don't worry,' she laughed. And I refrained from telling her she was heading headlong for disaster.

That wasn't the only thing I didn't tell Art. I said nothing, even to Shirley, about my new friend, Andy. The first time we met up was for coffee, but as the hours passed coffee became dinner, and dinner became a gig in a pub on the quays. Dublin hadn't seen so much of me in years.

Andy told me about her father who had dementia and about her sister who belonged to a church and hadn't spoken to Andy since she'd told her she was gay. She told me about the woman she'd lived with for six years, and how that woman's jealousy had destroyed what they'd had, and that what they'd had had been very good for the most part, but that she couldn't live in a cage. That was how she'd felt, she said. Caged. And wasn't coming out supposed to be the opposite of that? Wasn't it all about liberation? I said I guessed it was and I grew reticent when she asked me about Art and Louise. Come on, she said. I want to know everything. And as the evening went on, she did.

A week later we met in the Phoenix Park. Andy wanted to rent bikes and cycle round all three hundred acres. I hadn't been on a bike in years, and she laughed when I told her about how my grandmother had once run a woman into a ditch, she was that dangerous on a bicycle, and how my mother, who was quiet, said the madness skipped a generation. She said she could understand my mother's fears as I wobbled off ahead of her, and she told me to watch out for the herd of deer grazing a good kilometre away.

I was lying in the grass, Andy stretched next to me, one hand shielding her eyes, when she told me she was going back to Boston.

'When?' I said, quietly. Surprised by the way my stomach plummeted at her words.

'Saturday. My sister got in touch to say dad's had a stroke. She can't manage on her own – what with dad and the kids. You know ... she didn't ask me a single thing about myself. That's how I know it's bad – she'd never have spoken to me otherwise.'

I felt in the grass for Andy's hand, squeezed her callused fingers in mine as the sun beat down on our faces.

'I'm sorry,' I said, not knowing quite what it was I was sorry for; her sister's attitude, her dad's decline, or the fact that she was leaving. 'Will you come back?' I said.

Andy sighed. 'I want to. But whether I'll be able to is another thing ...'

She ran her thumb back and forth across my knuckles tracing the bones beneath my skin. And a voice told me that it was a good thing she was going away. As it was, I was teetering on the edge of madness.

When I got home, Art was in the kitchen washing up. 'Where have you been?' he said. 'Shirley called – I thought you two were together.'

'No, no. I forgot my phone,' I said, guilt, like a vice, squeezing my insides. Had he read our messages? And if he did, what would he make of the thread between me and Andy? There was the chance, of course, that Art would think that Andy was an Andrew and the thought was enough to make me laugh – before I wondered sadly if anyone ever knew another person at all. Such was the irony of our situation.

Days passed without any word. It was on the Friday night, the eve of her departure, as I sat watching *Ozark* with Art, that my phone pinged with a message. 'Will I pause?' Art said. 'No, it's fine. I'm sure it's nothing important.' Louise had come home that evening and was flaked on the couch next to me. I'd seen her check her phone several times, then throw it on the seat beside her. She'd grabbed it up, thinking it was hers when my phone went, and for one crazy moment I felt like telling her that I knew what it was like – this waiting.

It had been a crazy few days, Andy said. She'd had to move her stuff from the flat in order to sub-let it. Luckily, she had a friend who'd agreed to keep her things in his spare room until she got back. She'd put a smiley face after that, and I wondered how serious she was about returning. And if she did, what then? Art and I had a good life, and there was Louise to consider. She was all for women's rights, but how would she react to her mother coming out? I wasn't Shirley. I couldn't simply walk out of one life and into another. Particularly when that other was not a given.

Andy had not proclaimed any great feelings for me. There *was* something, I'd felt it when she held my hand, it was there in the way she looked at me. But things could often be mistaken for more than they actually were. It was more than twenty years ago since I'd made a fool of myself by mistaking the chemistry between friends for something more; forgivable at twenty, less so at forty.

I looked at Art slumped in the armchair, eyes on the screen, and I wondered if he had his secrets too. There was that one time when I'd seen over his shoulder a message from an ex. She said she didn't know if it was because Bowie had died, but she couldn't get him out of her mind. And given that Art possessed every album Bowie had recorded, I supposed that wasn't so unusual. I had no idea what Art's response was. I was so sure that he wasn't the cheating type I hadn't dwelled on it. But maybe we all have it in us; this ability to compartmentalise. What I felt for Andy had nothing to do with Art. It was something else entirely.

A new restlessness crept in. I met Shirley and half-listened to her exploits. The affair with the Brazilian had started to wane. Incredible as he was in bed, his imperfect English was beginning to grate; in particular how he added an extra syllable to every word that ended in 'ed'. 'If he tells me one more time that he work-ed,' she said, 'I'll go crazy.' She was thinking of quitting the salsa class and taking up the Argentine tango.

The first message came a week after Andy had flown home. Her father had been in bad shape when she arrived, to the extent that they didn't know if he would recover, but in the last couple of days he'd shown signs of improving. Things were strained with her sister, who didn't want to put their father in a nursing home, but was adamant that she couldn't take care of him either. The way the sister saw it, Andy was single and therefore she ought to be the one to step up and look after him.

I didn't have siblings and I told Andy that I'd always thought I'd have liked a sister until I'd met Art's. Noreen was a primary school teacher who talked to Art like he was still a schoolboy. Mind you, it wasn't just Art, Noreen had a way that always made you feel that she was assessing you. It didn't help that most of her sentences began with 'do you not think ...' Until I'd turned around one day and said 'believe it or not, Noreen, sometimes I do.'

The messaging became nightly. Andy told me about her father teaching her guitar, and how she played her first gig with him when she was just fifteen. I told her about my first boyfriend who was a drummer and how I blamed him for a string of crushes on musicians in the years that followed. 'And what about Art – does he play?' she asked. I told her the only thing Art played was soccer and a bit of squash. But she did approve of his obsession with Bowie.

Then one evening she told me she'd arranged to meet up with Alice, the ex that she'd lived with for six years. She'd run into her in the street and they'd got talking. She was meeting her for a drink in a bar in the neighbourhood where they used to live. It was nice chatting to her, she said, she'd forgotten how funny Alice was. 'Wasn't she the possessive one?' I said, and immediately regretted how petty that sounded.

I woke at three in the morning and couldn't get back to sleep. Andy was somewhere in a bar now with this Alice –

the woman she'd shared her life with, who knew her so much better than I did. I imagined them laughing over old times – skirting round the problems that had driven them apart. Would Alice invite her back to her place – to their place? And would Andy be lonesome enough to go? Lying on my back in the dark, I wondered how it would be with a woman, to taste her as Art used to taste me – something he hadn't done in a long time. Something I thought might come back when Louise left for university, but celibacy had become our new norm and it was difficult to find our way back.

Most of the girls I knew had experimented with other women. I remembered one night in a club when a drunk girl had pinned me up against the toilet wall and kissed me, I'd pushed her off and asked her what she thought she was doing. When I told Shirley she'd laughed and told me I should have tried it. 'Have you?' I said. Shirley shrugged and said who hadn't? There *were* fantasies. Sometimes I imagined myself going to a bar and taking up with a stranger just to try it. It wouldn't feel like cheating – cheating was something you did with another man. This would be a one-off caper. Something that may even have turned Art on, if he'd known. But I never told him. And I never did it.

I went through the next day zombified, checking my phone like a teenager for any updates on how Andy's night had gone, but according to WhatsApp she hadn't been online in twelve hours, and all remained quiet on Facebook. For the first time in a month, Andy didn't message me that night. It was Art's squash evening, so I tried to distract myself by reading a book – but when I'd read the same page five times I decided it was time to give up. Instead, I rang Shirley – and though it hadn't been my intention, my dilemma somehow spilled out.

Typically, Shirley was more affronted at my not having told her than shocked by my exposé. 'And this has been going on since the gig,' she said. 'All this time?'

'I'd hardly say going on,' I said. 'Nothing has been *going on.*' I found myself speaking in hushed tones. Even though Art was out, paranoia ensured I had one eye on the door.

'No, but you'd like it to by all accounts.'

'I don't know. I don't know what I'd like. Anyway, it doesn't look like I have anything to worry about now. Andy's in Boston. And she met up with her ex last night. She may not come back at all.'

'But you want her to?' Shirley said. 'I mean, let's say this is mutual, and she said she'd come back if *you* wanted her to, what would you do? Would you leave Art for this woman?'

'No. I don't know,' I said, beginning to regret having said anything. Rather than clarifying anything, all it had done was to raise more questions.

'Jesus, you're actually thinking about it,' she said.

And I couldn't find the words to deny it.

Two days passed without any contact from Andy. There were no updates. No evidence of her having been online. I was short-tempered, snapping at Art over stupid things like buying tinned mackerel instead of sardines in the supermarket. Everything he did irritated. Shirley texted asking if I'd made a decision. But I felt more than ever that the matter was not mine to decide. That maybe it never had been.

It was a simple ping that put an end to my bad mood.

I'm sorry I fell off the planet. My dad died on Saturday night. Another stroke, he just wasn't strong enough to pull through this time. It's a strange feeling with both my parents gone – it's like I've been cast adrift, which might sound ridiculous at my age. Christ, I'll be fifty next year! But you know what I mean, it's just us now – me and Ivy are the generation. Things are tense there, of course. You'd think with losing dad we could put our differences aside, but no, she's as critical as always, sniping every chance she gets. But I won't rise to the bait, for my own sanity at least. I just need to get through this.

Saturday night. It was the afternoon, Boston time, when I'd last heard from Andy. That same evening she was supposed to meet Alice.

Soon as dad's funeral is over, I'll be on a plane. There's nothing here to hang around for. If I'm honest, I can't wait to get back to Dublin. I expect I'll be there within the week ...

Andy was coming back. It was only a matter of days. I began to text Shirley, then changed my mind. I'd tell her in my own time. Just because Andy was returning it didn't mean she was coming back for me. She'd made a life here long before I'd turned up at that gig.

It wasn't long before the initial adrenaline became anxiety. What if I'd misread Andy's warmth, if all she wanted was a friend? Would the relief be more than the disappointment? Could I go on as I had been with Art and never say a word? Would I be satisfied with that? Of course, the other outcome brought a different set of anxieties. There would be the conversation to have with Art. The news to break to Louise. I'd already started having these imaginary conversations with them both. One day I missed my turn off the motorway on my way to work. Another morning I jumped sky high when Art appeared behind me in the bathroom mirror as I stood brushing my teeth. 'Are you ok?' he asked. And I knew that he knew something was up. But I smiled and told him I was fine, that I just hadn't slept well the previous night.

Andy disappeared again, but this time I didn't worry. There were the funeral arrangements to make, her sister to deal with, the ceremony itself. I'd been through this with my own father and I knew she wouldn't have a minute. I sent her a message, telling her that there was no need to reply, but that I hoped she was ok, and I looked forward to seeing her whenever she felt up to it. I added kisses before pressing send.

The next day I got a message on WhatsApp.

So, you'll never guess where I am? Sitting in the departure lounge waiting for my flight to be called. Should touchdown in dear old Dublin tonight just after seven.

Really? Great, I wrote back. *I live twenty minutes from the airport. Why don't you let me pick you up instead of waiting on a bus?*

Would you? Oh my God, that would be great. Hope you've got space for all these cases.

She sent me the flight number and the approximate arrival time. I wondered where she was going to stay since she'd sub-let the flat. Neither of us had banked on her coming home so quickly.

'Well, look at you all done up,' Art said. 'Where are we off to then? Or is it still a surprise?'

'What do you mean?' I said. No sooner had the words left my mouth that I remembered; today was Art's birthday. Every year, for the last two decades I'd brought him some place new, never telling him where we were going until we were in the car, sometimes not until we got there. But now I couldn't even fake remembering. There would never be enough time to eat out and get to the airport.

'Oh, Art. I'm really sorry,' I said.

'What? You actually forgot?'

'No, of course not. I thought it was tomorrow. I ...'

Art shook his head. 'Well, the times really are a-changing,' he said. 'So where are you off to – out gallivanting with Shirley, I suppose.'

His tone irked me even though I was in the wrong – no, it irked me *because* I was in the wrong.

'If you must know I'm collecting a friend from the airport.'

'Oh yeah, which friend?'

'You don't know her, someone I met through Shirley.'

'Right, well. I guess we'll do it tomorrow then – if you *have* booked somewhere, that is.'

'Jesus, Art, is it such a big deal?'

He turned in the doorway, and the way he looked at me made me regret my outburst. 'Not in itself, no, but I don't know what's going on with you these days. You're different. It's like you're not even here most of the time. I might be out of line here, and I don't want to sound like some jealous prick, but is there someone else? All this checking your messages – this goofy smiling to yourself – this ... vacancy ... it's not like you. I'd rather know if I'm being made a fool of.'

'Art, no. There isn't anyone else.' *Yet.* 'But you're right, things are different. But it's not just me – I mean ... look at us – we're not really a couple anymore, are we? We're two people living in the same house, we have been for years. Do you never think maybe there's more than this?'

'What do you mean more than this – this is a marriage, isn't it? I don't know what's got into you – is it Shirley? Has Shirley leaving Mike given you itchy feet, is that it?'

'It's nothing to do with Shirley. I can make up my own mind. It's ... I just wonder sometimes if we wouldn't be better off living separate lives?

Art shook his head. 'I can't believe this.'

Neither could I. I couldn't believe I'd come out with it. The conversation was nothing like what I'd had in my head. In my head it was all platitudes.

'Look, let's not do anything hasty here. Ok, we may have gone a bit off track, but can't we talk about it?'

I nodded. I had to give him something. 'Of course. Not now though, I'll be late. Her plane gets in at seven.'

'What time will you be home?'

'I'm not sure. But we'll talk, I promise.'

I got to the airport early, checked the arrivals board and saw that her plane had been delayed by half an hour. I was both shaken and exhilarated by the talk with Art. It was a talk that we needed to have; it had simply been precipitated by my forgetting his birthday. That and my feelings for Andy.

I took the escalator to the first floor and ordered a coffee. A decision I regretted after the first few sips, my nerves were already on end and the caffeine just added to the angst. I took out my phone to pass the time, saw that I had missed a call from Louise and I dialled into the voicemail. 'What's up with dad?' she said. 'Seems in bad form. I thought you two would be out for his birthday! Anyway, I hope everything's alright. I'll be home at the weekend. Better pick something up for the old grouch.'

Louise. What would she think of my predicament? She'd always been a daddy's girl. And I dreaded the thought that she'd take Art's side despite that she thought herself so liberal. I didn't want it to be a big thing. Surely, we could get on with it and be friends even? There were other couples who managed it – who even dined out with their respective partners. I imagined Andy and me sitting across a table from Art and some woman. But no – actually, I couldn't imagine it. Somehow the thought bothered me.

I left half the coffee and headed back down to the arrivals hall, which was crowded with families and strangers holding signs with names printed in capital letters. Andy's plane would have landed by now. I pictured her standing by the carousel, poised to grab these cases she'd mentioned. She must have brought a lot of her stuff from Boston. She'd said in one of her messages that

Ivy was keen to put their father's house on the market and I guessed she'd had to clear out her things.

It was impossible to miss her with her blue hair. She came out among a group of people, eyes scanning the crowd, wheeling an oversized case, guitar strapped on her back. She smiled and raised a hand when she saw me.

'Boy, are you an angel,' she said. 'I don't know how we'd manage this lot if you hadn't come. Mia, this is Alice,' she said, turning to introduce the woman who'd walked out several paces behind her, struggling with two cases that suggested anything but a short stay. Alice smiled, or maybe grimaced, it was hard to tell. Andy hugged me, and I plastered a smile on my face as the phone buzzed in my pocket.

'Will you be staying long, Alice?' I said.

Rupture

What was I doing when my brother died? That precise moment when his body crumpled to the ground and failed to rise again. Did it happen as I stood to answer the shrill buzz of the intercom? Was he already falling as I jogged lightly down the stairs from our first-floor apartment to open the door to the pizza delivery girl?

I picture his last moments on a split screen – there's Neil laying our places at the table, my brother exchanging banter in the locker room before he runs onto the pitch; face lit, ignorant of the hand that fate is about to play. The weight of the coins in my fist as I pass them to the girl; the rattle as she drops them in the pocket of her sky-blue hoodie. It's as I turn to climb the stairs, as Neil lights the candle and uncorks the wine, that a teammate turns in confusion, wondering why he didn't see the tackle that's brought my brother down. A life snuffed out in the minutes it's taken for that transaction between me and a pizza delivery girl.

Ali's call was the first sign, phone vibrating amid the detritus of leftover pizza causing the dog, dozing on my knee, to kick up a rumpus as though she knew the news wasn't good. By the time I reached it, it had stopped its din. 'It's Ali,' I said, amid Scout's barking. 'Ali? At this hour of the night?' Neil's eyes rounded as he stooped to hush the dog. Ali at any hour would be strange; it had been almost three years since we'd spoken. Three years since my brother had ordered her not to answer my calls. And even as I tapped call back, I wondered whether it wasn't a mistake.

Ali picked up on the third ring, voice muffled like she had a head cold. *Debs, oh Debs* was all she managed before her voice cracked and her mother's cut in. I listened as Mrs Dillon reported, as she might to any stranger, what she knew. Kian had collapsed on the pitch during GAA practice. Attempts to defibrillate him had failed. It was instant, they said.

By the time the ambulance had arrived, he was already gone. And in some detached part of my brain, I thought that was my kid brother alright, never one to hold back on an invitation.

When Neil asked if I wanted to see him, I shook my head. It wasn't as if my brother awaited a reconciliation on his deathbed. I couldn't shake the image of him in his club jersey stretched on a slab in the hospital morgue as he surely would be until the undertaker came to claim him. And what then? There was the funeral to get through. Ali's hand to hold if she'd let me. But would she let me? Or would she stay fast to my brother's wishes never to speak to me again.

Neil sat next to me until I told him to go to bed; there was no point in both of us losing a full night's sleep. When, half an hour later, I slipped the harness over Scout's muzzle, and heard Neil snore as I paused outside the bedroom door, I envied him his oblivion.

The apartment block was shrouded in silence. In the stairwell the ghost of myself and that delivery girl lingered as I released the door and stepped into the night. We crossed the road, Scout leading, passed the deserted playground where Kian had rocked Albert, my nephew, back and forth on the swings last time they'd visited. Albert was seven now. I still sent cards on birthdays and Christmas; I ordered gifts from Amazon, which were neither acknowledged nor returned. I imagined him sprouting into a boy, but since Kian had unfriended me on Facebook, I was deprived of witnessing even that virtual transition.

Scout tugged on the lead. On the beach, I let her off and she scampered down to the shore and sniffed her way along its edge. I ambled behind, eyes drawn to the cargo ships way out at sea, and I thought of Ali who was surely awake too. On impulse, I sent a text, though I expected no answer. I was surprised minutes later when the reply came. *My heart is shattered*, was all she said.

It was through me that Kian and Ali had met, and because of that I've always felt somewhat responsible. Ali and I crossed paths several months before when I responded to an advert on a Meetup group. She was running a yoga retreat in a centre in the midlands – somewhere so remote that it didn't feature on any bus route. When I told her I had no car, she said it wasn't a problem. She lived in the city centre and if it was convenient, she'd pick me up in Merrion Square.

She arrived in a little yellow Punto stacked to the ceiling with yoga mats looking slightly dismayed when she saw the size of my travel bag. 'Moving house?' she teased. 'No, but it looks like you are.' We both laughed as I squeezed into the passenger seat and propped my feet on my bag.

She told me she was just back from India where she'd been upgrading her yogi skills. In her ethnic trousers and black vest top she looked every bit the part. But it was her tawny dreadlocks that impressed me most – that and the tiny diamond that twinkled in her nose. She hadn't always been a yogi, she said. She'd been a bank teller before that.

Her announcement that she was throwing up a pensionable job was enough, for her father at least, to bring on an attack of angina. 'There's more to life than being stuck behind a counter all day,' she said, as we hurtled down the M4, her bracelets tinkling as she tapped her fingers in time to a tune on the radio.

From that weekend on, Ali and I were inseparable. When Kian ran into us in a café, gatecrashed our coffee and added my new friend on Facebook, I admitted to apprehension. Girls found Kian disarming, and Ali was no exception. But I knew the speed with which my brother tired of his conquests. It took time to see the other side of him – the moody, impatient side. The side that said if you didn't agree with his views, you were wrong, plain and simple. We clashed over many things, Kian and I, but we both loved Ali and so I'd been prepared to give him the benefit of the doubt.

I considered missing the wake. Instead, arriving at the church late on the day of the funeral and taking a seat near the back so that I wouldn't have to speak to anyone, but Neil said that would be even more conspicuous. And besides, I had nothing to be ashamed of – nothing to hide. I'd have been willing to park the whole disagreement – it was Kian who'd refused to.

Cars lined both sides of the road and we had to park almost a block away. There was a moment when I almost told Neil to keep on driving. The front door was open and as we walked up the driveway two small boys came careering out – one of them was wearing what looked like his communion suit, and bore such a likeness to my brother, as he shouted and grinned gap-toothed at his friend, that I faltered. It was, of course, Albert.

People were congregated in the hallway. Two of my brother's friends, who he'd known since he was a boy offered me their condolences. They knew nothing of the rift of course, Kian never being someone to broadcast his business. 'Jesus, I couldn't believe it. It was so sudden,' one of the men said, and I nodded and said something about still not having really taken it in.

The room was full of people I half-knew; as well as neighbours; strangers and a few stray relations who shook my hand and asked me what had happened. 'Was it a heart condition?' one woman asked. 'Didn't your poor father die of a stroke?' A heart condition. *A condition of the heart.* The words swirled in my head. 'I don't know,' I said, as I brushed past her towards the conservatory where they'd laid my brother out – and where Ali was standing by the head of his coffin.

'You came,' she said, her hand going to her mouth when she saw me. Her mother patted my arm and shook Neil's hand. And to avoid looking at my brother, I embraced Ali.

It was only when she drew back and swiped a hand across her eyes that I allowed myself to look at him. At first, I didn't think he resembled himself. He looked thinner, had grown a beard, and his mouth was drawn in a thin line by the undertaker. Arms round each other Ali and I stared down at him, and it was then that Albert entered the room. He looked at me, shyly at first, but then recognising me, he smiled. And it was that smile, so like Kian's, that broke my heart.

'You didn't answer my messages,' I said to Ali.

'I couldn't – you know what he's like. Answering would have been taking your side.'

'My side?' It was just then that I saw her through the doorway – Naoise Quinn – handing round a platter of sandwiches as if she were a hostess at a party. 'What's she doing here?' I said.

Ali's gaze tracked mine. 'Who? Naoise? Her and Kian were great friends. She's been very good helping to organise everything.'

An image of my brother upstairs in this house – pre-Christmas drinks – Neil and I not quite as out of it as the rest of them. I'd stumbled upon them, my brother and Naoise, kissing, his hands inside her blouse, and her giggling saying that someone might come, someone might see them.

I'd called him the next day, told him if he didn't tell Ali, that I would – and he'd said, before slamming the phone down, that I'd tell her over his dead body. After that he wouldn't take my calls. Ali wouldn't answer my calls either. And I had no idea what he'd told her to turn her against me.

In the end it was Albert that stopped me. I'd driven over to the house with the intention of telling Ali – but as I drove into the housing estate, I spotted them.

My brother was crawling round the grass with Albert on his back and the two of them were laughing. They didn't see the car and so I drove right on past, circled the block and on towards home. Kian loved that boy. Would it be right to wrench them apart – even if it were my brother's fault? I'd just have to hope that in catching him, I'd put a stop to anything that might materialise between my brother and Naoise Quinn.

Neil hung back, discreetly allowing me the time I needed alone with my sister-in-law. He was talking now to an elderly aunt that I hadn't seen since our wedding.

'I guess you didn't tell Neil,' Ali said.

'Tell him what?'

'About what happened that night at the party.'

'You mean you know?' I said.

Ali nodded. 'He said he'd never speak to you again if you didn't tell him. He always had a lot of time for Neil. I did too. I do – but maybe you were right not to say anything. You're still together.'

I looked at Ali, lost for words. So that was what my brother had done, turned the situation on its head; made me the guilty one and Neil the cuckold. Kian – never wrong, always self-righteous. Over my dead body, he'd said. And there she was: Naoise Quinn, sandwiches held aloft, weaving ever closer.

MONGO

'My mother's got a new boyfriend,' Sylvia tells me.

I'm sprawled on her bed, a love songs compilation cassette playing, while Sylvia, knees drawn up, cotton wool between her toes, deftly applies varnish to her nails. In the background, Meatloaf declares that two out of three ain't bad.

'He's some shit,' I say.

'What? You've met him?' Sylvia wrinkles her nose and stares at me hard, eyes huge behind round lenses.

I shake my head. 'He wants her, he needs her, but there ain't no way ...'

'You haven't been listening to a thing I've said, have you?' she says.

I admit that I haven't. I've been thinking about Avril Monaghan and what a traitorous bitch she is, and that no one else can see it except Sylvia and me.

Today was the first day back after the summer holidays, and I'd been dreading it. Earlier that summer Ronan Daly had finally asked me out after a two-year cat and mouse game, only to end it a few weeks later without so much as a by-your-leave.

We'd all been part of the same group: Ronan and his pal Dylan, Avril Monaghan, Ciara Fogarty, Aisling Ryan and me since first year. Avril and I weren't really friends, we just happened to have all the others in common. Sylvia wasn't part of this clique, she was in the B stream, not that she was any less clever than us, but that she had so many responsibilities at home she didn't have time to study. After school, I'd call over to Sylvia's house, but it was the others whose company I kept all day.

That morning, I'd arrived to find the girls sitting in the alcove outside room 2.1. Avril Monaghan was holding court, Ciara and Aisling on either side of her. There was no sign of the boys. Avril smiled sweetly and asked how the rest of my summer had been. I hadn't seen her since July because she'd been staying with cousins, but I knew well that she'd heard all about the break-up. 'Fine,' I shrugged, and Avril smiled disinterestedly. 'I was just telling the girls,' she said. 'I was at my cousin's wedding last week. Ronan came as my date.'

Aisling had the decency to look embarrassed, whether for me or for Avril's bombshell I couldn't tell. I smiled tight-lipped and said nothing. I knew Avril had as much interest in Ronan as I had in Bridget Monroe, who sat beside me in every art class and was rumoured to have a thing for petite brunettes, though no one had ever actually seen anything to prove it. No, Avril's bombshell was designed for no other reason than to rile me. Ronan was just a pawn in her game.

Sylvia wiggles her toes and clicks off the cassette killing Phil Collins' Groovy Kind of Love, which is just as well because it isn't lifting my mood any. 'C'mon, let's get out of here,' she says. I follow her down the stairs, she stops to take an orange from the fruit bowl on the kitchen table – lobs one to me and we're almost out the door when her mother calls from the front room, asking if we can take care of Robbie for the evening. Sylvia gives me a look, half-apologetic, half-resigned and goes upstairs to get her brother.

Sylvia's mother is a beauty therapist who works in a salon in the local shopping centre. She packs Robbie off to the John of Gods in the mornings, and in the afternoons it's Sylvia who meets him off the bus and takes care of him until her mother gets home. Sylvia's mother works Saturdays too, and so we usually take Robbie out somewhere – to the park or the shopping centre, or if Sylvia manages to guilt her mother into it, she gives us money to go to the cinema.

This evening, it's clear that Sylvia's mother has plans. She's wearing the fake tan they do in the salon; her lips are frosted pink and her eyelashes appear to have doubled in length. 'Going anywhere nice?' I ask her. She smiles. 'Rafferty's on the Green,' she says. I nod, though I haven't a clue where she means. It must be one of those posh places like the one my father brought my mother to for her fortieth birthday because she'd complained they never went anywhere.

Just as we're on our way out the door, Robbie lagging after us, a blue sports car, something never seen in our estate, comes careering up the road and stops abruptly outside the house. The door opens and a man gets out. 'Hey Sylvia, is your mom inside?' His lips draw back in a wide, one-dimpled smile that does something funny to my insides. His hair, blonde like the Bros brothers, is combed back and he wears blue jeans and a navy shirt. Sylvia jerks her head towards the door. 'Yeah, she should be ready,' she says.

'Who's that?' I ask, as soon as he's vanished into the house.

'My mother's new boyfriend,' Sylvia says, taking Robbie by the hand to cross the road. 'That's what I was trying to tell you earlier. Only you'll never guess who he is.' She gives me a pointed look over her glasses.

'Who?' I ask.

'Only Avril flipping Monaghan's father.'

I stall on the pavement to look back at the house. 'You're kidding me?' I say.

'Nope.'

All I can think is it's as well she didn't get her father's looks, or Avril would be an even bigger pain in the backside than she already is.

Some woman's yellow hair has maddened every mother's son. Avril's swapped seats with Dylan so she can sit next to Ronan in English class. She smiles over when she catches me looking, then turns to whisper something in Ronan's ear and giggles. Dylan seems none-too-happy about the arrangement either, and I think maybe it's because we're friends – until I criticise her and he jumps to her defence. Turns out he's just sorry it's not him she's chosen to play her little games with.

'I don't even know what they see in her,' I complain to Sylvia. 'She's ... mousy.'

I'm not being a bitch, it's true. Avril's got this gorgeous wavy blonde hair, but her smile is nothing like her father's. Instead she's got two tiny rows of milk teeth and a witchy little chin. Still, as my mother always says, there's no accounting for taste. And it's the flattery that does it.

Avril hangs off Ronan, but she does it with Dylan too, and it doesn't mean anything. She'll link her arm through the boys' when she's walking home from school, play with their hair in a way that would embarrass them if she was their mother. She does it with the girls too, has a way of making them feel special. She's even turned the charm on me in the past if only for the benefit of the others.

'What's he like?' I ask Sylvia, expecting her to bag out Avril's father. Not because of Avril, but because she never likes her mother's boyfriends.

'He's actually nice,' she says. 'He's taking Robbie and me go-karting on Saturday. I'm sure you can come too.'

There isn't room for us all in Padraic's blue sports car – he's told us to call him Padraic, not Mr Monaghan – so Sylvia's mam drives us and he takes Robbie. I know Sylvia's impressed by this because her mother's other boyfriends high-tailed it soon as they learned there was a downs syndrome son.

Padraic pays for us all. I tell him my parents gave me money, but he insists. Then he gives me that smile that makes you feel like the sun's just come out. I can't believe Avril's father is so nice. Her mother, I think, must be a right cow. It's no wonder he left them.

We get into our boiler suits, stick our helmets on and it feels like we're going to the moon. Sylvia's mother looks gorgeous, like Kylie Minogue in Neighbours. It's amazing how some women look even better in overalls.

The man from the track is showing us how to operate the go-karts. There's an accelerator and a brake, nothing too complicated. Padraic spends time with Robbie making sure he understands it. He tells Sylvia's mother not to worry, that he'll stay close to him.

And then I see them hurrying towards us. Avril Monaghan with Ronan in tow. 'So sorry we're late, it was my fault,' she tells her father breathlessly. She stands on her tiptoes to kiss his cheek, then introduces Ronan, who looks mortified.

As Avril is busy sizing up Sylvia's mother, he turns to me. 'Look, I'm sorry, I didn't know you'd be here,' he says.

'Are you and her ...'

'No – we're just friends.' He blushes though when he says it, and even if it's true, which I doubt, then it's obvious he's hanging on hoping for more.

'I never knew you had a brother, Sylvia,' Avril says, beaming at Robbie. 'He's so cute.'

Robbie stares at her, transfixed.

'You two had better get a move on,' Padraic says. 'We can't stand around here all day.'

Avril looks great in her red boiler suit, blonde curls hanging down beneath the helmet. In fairness, she looks pretty when she's not smiling – it's the teeth that let her down.

Ronan goes to help her into the go-kart, but she tells him she can manage. Maybe he could help me, she says, knowing full-well the awkwardness between us. She smiles as if she's just done me this huge favour. Sylvia is furious about the whole thing.

'Why didn't he tell us she was coming?' she mumbles.

I shrug. 'Suppose he just wants you all to be one big happy family.'

And it was clear he didn't know about Ronan. He looked just as surprised as the rest of us to see him tagging along.

Avril's got in the go-kart next to Sylvia's mother's. They're talking and just before Avril takes off she says something that makes her frown.

Suddenly, we're all on the move. I power the accelerator not wanting to be left behind. Avril leaves us for dust, zips past her father with Ronan close behind. I slow down to check on Robbie who's way behind and having some difficulty steering. He's turning the wheel from side to side like a kid in a computer arcade, but he's definitely got the hang of the accelerator. Avril's out of sight now – tearing up the track so fast it's only a matter of time before she overtakes us. Padraic's trying to tell Robbie to pull over, but he doesn't seem to hear.

It happens behind me. I hear nothing but the bang and the shouts. The staff from the go-karting company run onto the track waving for everyone to stop. I turn to see Robbie's kart turned sideways, and Avril's swivelled into the barrier. She's not hurt though, because she's jumped out of the kart and is screaming at him. Poor Robbie looks devastated.

She pulls her helmet off and hurls it at him. It hits his shoulder, his reflexes too slow. 'Fucking retard,' she screams. 'What were you doing – trying to run me off the track? It's all your fault anyway,' she says. Screaming now at her father who's asking Robbie if he's ok. 'What do you expect when you bring a bloody mongo along?'

Everyone's silent. Sylvia's got her arm around Robbie and is leading him away. Ronan, who had rushed to Sylvia's aid, is mortified enough not to meet my eye. Padraic says something to Avril – and her face crumples. 'I'm sorry. It was the shock was all. You know I didn't mean it. I didn't,' she says, as he turns his back on her to apologise to Sylvia's mother who looks fit to kill.

'Pack of fucking retards,' Avril says, as she stalks off the track. But no one is listening anymore.

NOBODY NEEDS TO KNOW

When the Keoghs came to view number nine, my mother said the house was unlucky on account of what had happened to the Gaffneys. But rather than being put off, Caroline Keogh stood on our doorstep, invited herself in for tea and said she didn't believe in superstition. My mother shrugged and put the kettle on.

Caroline Keogh sat on a stool at the breakfast bar, legs crossed, short denim skirt revealing badly painted legs, and listened, rapt, as my mother told her about how Mr Gaffney had lost control of the car one night and run into a concrete culvert. He'd survived it, but their five-year-old boy, Barry, had been killed instantly.

'Was he drunk?' Caroline Keogh wanted to know.

But my mother shook her head and told her that Mr Gaffney was one of those rare things: a tee-totaller. A man in absolute control of his life, until his eldest daughter, Marianne, arrived home one day to find him swinging from the oak tree in their backyard.

After the crash, no one had seen much of the Gaffneys. Not until Marianne came screaming out of the house that day and my father had rushed across to see what was wrong.

At school they said Marianne had gone funny. It was rumoured that she'd gone to stay in St Patrick's Hospital, and I didn't know if it was true or not, but a *For Sale* sign went up in the Gaffney's garden – and only a few months later, they were gone.

Marianne came to the house the day before they moved. I opened the door and was surprised to find her standing there. She indicated to a large sports bag at her feet. 'I was doing a clear out,' she said. 'Thought you might be interested in some of these. It's no hassle if you're not.' She stooped down to unzip the bag, and I saw that it was full of books. I wasn't much of a reader, but not wanting to offend her, I invited her in.

'No, thanks, I've to help my mother pack,' she said. 'Why don't you just take the bag? If there's anything you don't want, you might drop them into the Vincent de Paul ...'

I nodded and took the bag from Marianne's feet. We'd never talked much and I wondered why that was. But then she never talked much to anyone, and at school she had a reputation as a loner. That day, she paused walking down the path and turned. 'You could write to me,' she said. 'If you want.'

'I don't have your address,' I said.

'Well, maybe I'll write you.' She smiled before vanishing across the road.

The next day I went across to drop the bag back, but I could see through the curtainless windows that the house was empty and the Gaffneys were gone.

Things changed for me after the Keoghs arrived. For one thing, Mr Keogh, who ran a car showroom, gave me a job for the summer. Every morning, I went in and polished cars until they glistened in the showroom window. Then I vacuumed them inside. I loved the high-end models, the smell of leather and the gleam of the mahogany dashboards. I also had a regular number babysitting the Keogh kids, which provided me with more money for my beloved models. I had quite the collection of them, ranging from Renaults to Lamborghinis.

Amazingly, a letter came from Marianne. They'd moved to the countryside – and she loved it. All that peace, she said, the only noise for miles round was the cows. She could sit under a tree all day and read. Nothing else to bother her. I wrote back and told her about our new neighbours. It was the first letter I'd ever written. But the beginning of a keen correspondence.

I told Marianne that Caroline Keogh wasn't really my mother's type, and that I thought she felt sorry for her, which was why she entertained her anytime she called to the house. My mother, I knew, had an endless amount of empathy. 'How does she cope with all those children?' she'd said when the Keoghs moved in and we discovered there was a brood of seven. There was only my brother and me and I guessed we were enough to handle – particularly my brother who was still only eleven and always getting himself into scrapes.

Babysitting for the Keoghs became a regular thing. That might sound hard – looking after seven kids, but the youngest was six and they were stepping stones after that, so Mikey, the eldest, was only three years younger than me and when we managed to get the rest of them off to bed, we'd sit up and play computer games.

There were things I didn't mention in my letters to Marianne. Like the fact that Mr and Mrs Keogh weren't always out together. Or if they were, they'd come home separately. I preferred when Mr Keogh was there, he'd give me more money, and I'd get home straight away. Whereas when it was just Caroline, she'd pour herself a drink and expect me to sit and chat to her. Generally, during these conversations, Mrs Keogh – or Caroline – as she insisted I call her, berated her husband. The only thing he was good at, she said, was making money.

'We don't have sex anymore, Declan,' she told me one night. And I looked at my watch, anxious to get going. 'Why do you think that is?'

I shrugged, and she laughed and tapped her cigarette ash in a saucer. 'Guess he doesn't find me attractive anymore,' she said. 'I'm old. Suppose he thinks he can get with a young one. And who knows? Maybe he can. Why is it, do you think, that that's acceptable for men, but not for women?' She waved the cigarette around, ash dropping on the carpet as she slid her shoes off and kicked them under the coffee table.

'Come on. Let's sit down.' She flopped onto the leather couch where only a half hour before, Mikey and me had sat playing video games, and patted the place next to her. Reluctantly, I sat.

'Do I look old to you, Declan?'

'No. you're very attractive ...'

'I suppose a woman stops being sexy at a certain age,' she said.

I thought of the boys in the neighbourhood, about how they talked about the moms, and in particular about Mrs Keogh – Caroline. 'A lot of boys find you attractive,' I told her, blushing as the words came out. But she smiled and waved her cigarette around, blowing smoke out the corner of her mouth.

'Go on,' she said. 'You're just trying to make me feel better. I haven't had sex with my husband in a year, no ... more like two,' she said. 'Can you believe that? Not that I even want to. He's never been much good at it. Doesn't know the meaning of the word foreplay – just goes straight in for the kill. Sometimes I take his hand, try to show him what to do, but ... never mind ... Do you know what to do, Declan? Have you been with a girl yet?'

I shook my head, mortified, and looked at the door wishing Mikey would come in, but all was quiet upstairs.

'You should learn. You don't want to end up like Mal. Mal was a late starter – what you need to do is this,' she said. My eyes widened in panic as I tried to pull my hand from her surprisingly firm grip. Before I knew it, my palm was cupping hot, moist flesh. Caroline Keogh let out a heart-stopping moan, and terrified I yanked my hand from inside her blouse – a button pinging to the ground as I did so.

'I'm sorry, I have to go,' I said, forgetting my coat as I raced out the door, not hanging around for the money.

I avoided Mrs Keogh for a while after that. When my mother said she'd been over to ask if I could babysit the following weekend, I said no, that I was watching a football match with my friend Wayne. My mother gave me a funny look, knowing that I had zero interest in football.

I was in the showroom one day polishing the dash of an almost new Mercedes when a woman came in. She stood there, a leather bag hooked on one arm, looking around the showroom. The sales team were at lunch and so I wiped my hands on a cloth, stuck my head out the window and asked if I could help.

Up close, she wasn't as young as she appeared. A blonde ponytail and fake lashes did nothing to soften the hard lines around her mouth. She was wearing a shiny pink tracksuit top and leggings. 'No,' she said, looking around her, forehead creasing, as if wondering how she'd got there, or how I'd got there, and then Mal came out of the office beaming and whisked her out of sight. I thought of what Mrs Keogh said about Mal not knowing what to do to a woman.

The woman with the ponytail often turned up at the showroom after that. But she didn't look at cars. She and

Mal would smile and talk in low voices, and he'd disappear for an hour or maybe two and come back looking flushed. My experience with women extended only as far as my hand on Caroline Keogh's breast, but it didn't take a genius to see what was going on, and I figured the less I saw, the better it would be for everyone. I told Marianne about the ponytail lady in my letters, and she said it was obvious they were having an affair. By this stage we'd become regular pen friends – but I hadn't told her about Caroline Keogh or what had happened. Some things I just couldn't put into words.

One day I was sitting in an Alfa Romeo looking at magazines on my lunchbreak when I looked up to find Caroline Keogh gawking in the driver's window. I fumbled the magazine closed and looked desperately for somewhere to hide it. The cover, with a tanned, smooth-chested body-builder, did nothing to conceal the contents. And the way she looked at me, without saying anything, I knew she'd seen, and my faced blazed as I lowered the window.

'Sorry, Declan. I didn't mean to startle you,' she said, eyeing the bunch of car mags on the passenger seat, the one I'd had in my hand when she arrived so blatantly tucked beneath. 'Is Mal around?'

Mal had gone out about an hour before with the ponytailed blonde, and for reasons even I didn't know, I didn't want to drop him in it. At that moment, my guilt seemed linked with his, and I told her as far as I knew he'd gone over the northside and wouldn't be back for an hour at least. That way she wouldn't want to hang around. 'Never mind,' she said, and looked at me, eyes narrowed, before exiting just as quickly.

A few days later, my mother was pouring gravy over battered fish when she told me that Caroline wanted me to call over. 'I can't, I have homework,' I said.

'She said she needed you to help her with something, it wouldn't take long,' my mam said. 'You might just run over after dinner.'

I rang the bell and stood outside the porch, waiting. 'Declan, come in,' Caroline beamed. She was wearing that denim skirt she'd been wearing the first time I'd seen her. She was barefoot and I noted the botched leg tan didn't reach as far as her toes. A bracelet glinted on her left ankle.

'About the other day when I called by the showroom,' she started. 'I just wanted to let you know, I didn't tell anyone.'

I looked out the window, unable to meet her eye. I'd noted that the house was uncharacteristically quiet as soon as I'd entered and wondered where all the kids were. As if reading my mind, she waved a hand, gesturing toward the empty rooms. 'They're all gone to the nursing home to visit Mal's mother. Won't be home for ages yet. I thought you and I could talk – you know, adult to adult.'

'What about?' I said.

'Well, the magazines, and ... what happened the last time you were here, I didn't know you were, well, you know ... I haven't told anyone.'

She went to the sofa, ran her hand under the seats and pulled out a bunch of magazines. 'Mal's,' she said. 'He thinks I don't know about them.' I glanced at the covers, instead of bodybuilders, these ones contained pictures of women – women like Caroline Keogh, I thought, only younger.

'You don't like these ones? They don't do anything for you?'

I shook my head, cheeks fiery.

'We could help each other out, Declan,' she said, edging closer. 'It's like I said I haven't told anyone. I take it your parents don't know?'

I shook my head, miserably. The last thing I needed was Caroline Keogh marching over to our place telling my parents what she'd seen.

'Well, if you were to do me the odd little favour ... you wouldn't have to be into it or anything, you could look at those magazines, your ones, I mean, the ones you like and I could, well ... imagine what it is you might like one of those boys to do to you.'

Before I knew what was happening, Caroline Keogh had slid her hand onto my crotch.

'There see, it's not so bad, is it?' She tugged at my zipper, and I leapt back, pushing her hand away. 'I can't,' I said. 'It's not right.'

'Not right?' she scoffed. Then came at me again. And again, I thrust her hand away. I saw it then, the flint in her eyes, the downward turn of her mouth.

'Right, well, I suppose I might have to tell someone then, mightn't I? You see, I'm not too comfortable, Declan, with a boy like you looking after my kids, especially Mikey.'

'Mikey?'

'He's a good kid, an impressionable lad – and he thinks the world of you. If I were to say that you tried something ... inappropriate with Mikey.'

'What? I didn't. We played video games, that's all. Mikey's just a kid. I wouldn't ...'

'Oh, I know that,' Caroline Keogh said. 'But if I were to say otherwise ... who do you think the neighbours would believe? Your parents even if they heard about those dirty magazines? Mal wouldn't be too pleased either. You could be damn sure he wouldn't keep you on in the showroom. Not when he heard what you'd been up to in his precious cars!'

I stared at Caroline Keogh in disbelief. She wouldn't, would she?

'This is crazy. You know I'd never do anything to those kids ...'

'Oh, come on. There's no need to get wound-up now, Declan, is there? I didn't say I was *going* to tell anyone, did I? I mean, as long as you help me out, there's no need for anyone to know ... it's really none of their business, is it, the things we do?'

She stepped towards me; seized my hand in hers. I looked past her, out the window to the backyard, eyes drawn to the Gaffneys' oak tree. And in that moment, as she whispered the words in my ear, it was as though I could see him, Marianne's father, swaying in the breeze. 'Just think of your pictures, Declan,' she said. 'And leave the rest up to me.'

STORMS

She dreamt she rescued him from a flood. That the rain wouldn't stop, and the waters kept rising. Cars were swept down the street. Some had people inside, waving frantically out the windows, hands pressed to glass, mouths open.

Furniture bobbed by: a chair, followed by an ornate table. She dodged a grand piano that was headed straight towards them. One arm thrashing through the water as she pulled him with her, arm round his chest, desperately trying to keep him from going under.

First thing she did when she woke was go to the window. Pulled the curtains back to see black clouds blanketing the sky, but it was dry; that was something. She called him but got no answer.

Last winter, he'd gone up on the roof. Three tiles had come loose in a storm, and instead of getting someone in to fix it, he'd let the whole summer go by, and waited for the next bad forecast. 'I'm worried the whole roof's going to go,' he told her, as they'd stood back and surveyed the slates treacherous with moss. 'Don't you dare!' she said.

'I'll call someone.' There was that eerie stillness that prefaces a storm.

The next day she drove over there to find him on the lawn. He was lucky, nothing more than a busted arm. He'd been saved by that tree he was always threatening to cut down – the old Beech that blocked the light from the bedroom window.

She'd been having these dreams since she was a kid. Her husband said it was nothing but superstition – that no one could tell the future. When she'd dreamt the woman he'd been having an affair with, he'd said she was mad. Two months later, he was gone.

She didn't have breakfast that morning. Instead she took Jake, got in the car and drove the twenty miles to her father's place. She called him on the way, but he didn't answer. 'Come on,' she said. 'Come on.' Jake whined, and tried to climb on her lap as she sped at one twenty down the motorway. 'Down now,' she said. 'Good boy.' But the dog sensed there was something wrong.

The house was empty when she let herself in. Jake ran ahead of her, in and out of the empty rooms as she called her father's name. They found him at the end of the garden fencing up a hole in the hedge between him and the neighbours. 'You've got to stop worrying about me,' he told her. 'I'm fine.' She watched as Jake gambolled round his feet, along with Ruby, her father's old red setter.

'There was a flood,' she said. 'You were drowning.'

'Just like your mother,' he said, shaking his head. 'You know most of them came to nothing, don't you? She had these crazy dreams all the time. Not even five per cent hit the mark. The product of a restless mind, that's what it was. Your mother could never be easy.'

She followed him up the garden and back to the house, Jake jumping at the older dog, wanting to play. The old dog wagging its tail wanly, remembering a life before its arthritis.

The warning came. The weather woman pointed to swirling maps whose grey masses evolved in the background. You could barely make out the shape of the country covered as it was by all that cloud. 'A red warning has been issued for six counties,' she said. Teresa Mannion's video went viral again on YouTube reminding everyone of the gales that had battered Salthill, while barely a leaf was blown from a tree in Dublin and the city's shut-down was considered a farce. But how many of them remembered the woman who'd been killed when the bridge she was crossing was washed into a river? An isolated incident, they said. But weren't they all? Only the loved ones couldn't move on.

She dreamt of the red setter lying on the riverbank, its breathing laboured, fur sodden. When she woke, the rain was beating against the patio door.

Her father picked up on the third ring. His voice high as wind whooshed through the receiver.

'You're not out?' she shouted.

'God, no. Just down the garden checking everything's alright,' he said. 'Wind's destroyed the damn greenhouse. Bits of it all over the place. Found the plastic in next-door's garden torn to shreds.'

She nodded, stroked Jake curled on the sofa beside her. Earlier she'd taken him down to the beach despite the warning. She'd wanted to see the waves. A police car had driven the length of the promenade, telling people through a loudspeaker to clear the area, and she could see it, the tide coming in. She'd taken Jake and gone back inside. Restless, they'd played with a tennis ball in the apartment. The woman throwing, the ball ricocheting off the furniture, and the dog catching and bringing it back every time. She may have had her mother's restless mind, but it was her father's restless spirit made her hate being cooped up inside.

Her phone rang while she was watching the nine o'clock news. "Dad" flashing on the screen. But when she picked up, a woman's voice greeted her. She queried Veronica's identity, said she was calling from St James's Hospital, her father had been admitted to A&E. He was alright; a precaution really. Could she come?

He was propped up on a trolley in a corridor of the A&E department, a thin blue blanket draped over him. 'Get me out of here,' he told her. 'I'm fine.'

Wearing a flimsy gown, he looked as if he were awaiting a procedure and she was reminded of the time a few years before when she'd taken him in for a hernia operation and all he was worried about was the fact that his backside was on display.

'What happened?' she asked.

'Damn dog fell in the river. Went to the edge and got swept in. You should've seen it Ronnie, the water was right up the bank.'

A flash of the setter lying on the riverbank. Then her father carried by the swell.

'Veronica?' She turned to see a tall woman in a tweed jacket, plain black pants – a severely cut fringe like the actress from Pulp Fiction. She held out her hand. 'Doctor Field,' she said. 'Your father here's quite the hero.' Her lips curved in the hint of a smile. 'Only he's lucky to be here to tell the tale. Is he usually such a dare devil?' She glanced at a chart and gave Veronica a look that said she could only imagine what she had to put up with.

'When can I get out of here?' her father asked, ignoring the doctor's quip. Next to them a woman screamed repeatedly for a nurse. And the doctor ignored her.

'We'd like to hold on to you overnight – just as a precaution. Besides, where are you going to go dressed like that?' She turned to Veronica. 'He's going to need a change of clothes.'

Veronica nodded, pictured her father brought into the A&E, soaking wet. She wondered what had become of Ruby.

'Damn dog,' her father said. 'Slipped right in. What was I supposed to do?' He lowered his voice, although the doctor was already out of earshot. 'Bring me clothes, Ronnie, get me out of here.'

'Where's Ruby?' she asked.

'Richie's got her. It was Richie managed to pull us both out.'

Richie Barrett – like the weather himself, his moods were so sudden. He'd been like that since they were teenagers. But he loved her. She'd loved him back then too, even if his intensity frightened her. Richie was too much his own man. He'd drown her. And she was too much her own woman to ever allow that to happen.

'I'll go up to the house and get you some clothes,' she said. 'Then we'll see.'

'And you'll check on Ruby?' he called after her. The woman on the next trolley was still shouting for a nurse, but no one paid any attention.

She arrived to find Richie up a ladder, the big beech tree lying on the lawn and a massive hole in the roof.

'Just as well he wasn't in there,' he said. 'He might have been killed.'

He came down the ladder, stood next to her, and they both looked up at the damage.

'How's the dog?' she asked.

'She's in my place – stretched in front of the fire. Your father won't be coming back here tonight, not until we can get someone in to fix that. In truth, the whole roof needs to be done. No way it's going to withstand another storm. Suppose you dreamt it?' he said.

She looked to see if he was smiling, but his face was serious. He didn't mock her dreams like Carl had. He might have been more constant too. Unpredictability became predictable as the years passed. And youth burned into something more akin to calm.

They went inside. The roof had gone right through. Broken plaster and bits of tiles covered her father's unmade bed. It had broken the lamp on the bedside table. There was no question but that it might have got him, had he not been fool enough to venture out with the dog.

She set about cleaning up. Richie had gone back up on the roof. He said he'd try to fix some sheeting over the hole to keep the rain out. He'd get someone in first thing, a roofer friend, someone they both knew from their school days. It amazed her how much he'd stayed connected to the past.

He called her the next morning. She was getting breakfast ready, Jake circling her, eager for his kibble as her father snored in the spare bedroom. He slept until Jake managed to pry the door open and when he came out, he looked older than he did at home.

'You'll be happy to hear the roof's being fixed,' she told him, pouring his coffee. 'Richie's coming over later, he's going to bring Ruby.'

'There'll be no need for that,' he told her. 'Ring him and tell him I'll be home this morning. Save him a wasted journey.'

'What are you going to do?' she asked. 'Sleep under the stars?'

'It's only a hole, isn't it? We're not talking about a crater. I can sleep in the living room till it's fixed, fold out the old camp bed. I'll be alright.'

She looked at her father, tried to imagine what he'd do here all day. He'd be miserable. He needed space; the garden to tinker in, the old dog to walk. He'd never settle here, she knew that. He'd end his days in the house he'd been born in, and she had no intention of seeing him off anywhere else.

'Your mother's dreams,' he said, as they pulled up outside the house. 'They were right more times than I care to remember.'

The roofers had managed to do a patch-up job. The whole thing would need to be done in the summer, Richie told her, but for now, so long as they didn't have a bigger storm, it would hold.

'Didn't you two use to knock around together?' her father said, as the three of them sat at the kitchen table cradling mugs of tea.

'We did, yeah, when we were kids,' she said.

'She was always fierce stubborn,' Richie said. 'And bossy, she was always trying to boss me around.'

But when she looked at him, he was laughing.

'Takes after her mother,' her father said. 'Did she ever tell you about these dreams she has?'

'You'd be a fool not to heed them from what I hear.'

Richie winked at her. She smiled, stifling thoughts of last night's dream. Her father broke a Digestive biscuit, gave half to Ruby. The dream receded – a warm feeling in its wake. That was something she'd not be sharing with either of them.

INCENDIARY

Chloe was applying her make-up, as she did every morning on the train, when she learned of her husband's dilemma. Holding her mascara wand to her fluttering lashes, she stared at her reflection in the mirror, as the boys, clad in grey uniforms, descended on the carriage disturbing the reticent commuters.

'What d'ya think will happen with Mr Carty?' said a boy who had thrown himself into the seat next to her. Chloe's lashes fluttered before her compact.

Another boy who'd been studying a textbook looked up. Chloe could see him in the edge of the glass. 'I don't know. They're talking about Dunner getting back into school because of his background and all – but that would be weird, wouldn't it? I mean, you can't just loaf a teacher.'

Chloe dipped her forefinger in a pot of rouge, smeared it on her cheeks and pretended not to listen. A swift glance at the crest on the school jumper removed any doubt that it was Aiden they were talking about. She snapped her compact shut and stared out the window.

'He didn't loaf him but, did he? I heard it was a punch.'

'No, some of the fifth years were there and they said he loafed him. Anyway, Dunner's off his head. He shouldn't be let anywhere near the school.'

'I'd leave,' another boy said, 'if I were Mr Carty. The school board would be giving a license to lunatics like Pat Dunne if they let him back in after that.'

'Dunner used to be alright, but then his Da died and he lost it.'

A tall boy standing in the aisle spoke up. 'Pat Dunne was never alright. It's just now he can use his father's dying as an excuse. He was always a bully.'

'Well, I wish Carty'd come back. The sub's a disaster, hasn't a clue,' the boy with the textbook said.

'What have you got him for?'

'Maths. As if it wasn't difficult enough.'

Chloe watched the coast flash past the train window. She thought of Aiden leaving the house that morning, bag in hand – lips grazing her cheek as he told her he'd see her later. When did this incident happen? And why wasn't Aiden at work if the student had been suspended? Chloe took out her phone and dialled her husband's number. But then she changed her mind and hung up before it had a chance to ring.

Dunne. Had he mentioned the name before? She thought he had. Wasn't he the kid whose father had died in that horrible accident? It must have been almost a year ago. The train chugged along, jogging Chloe's hazy memory. Dunne. She was sure that was the name. She took out her phone again and typed 'Patrick Dunne' into Google. If the kid's name was Pat, chances were the father's was too. She paused and then added two more words: *death* and *fire*. She scrolled down the sites as the boys bundled out of the train at Aiden's station.

*

Aiden drove out to Killiney. He sat in the car, looked out to sea and waited for the train to pass carrying his wife and some of his students. Then he got out, threw his briefcase in the boot and walked down to the beach. It was after nine on a Thursday, he should have been teaching his first session of double maths, not here watching strangers and their dogs gambolling on the strand.

He'd told Mr Lavelle he needed time off after the incident. The principle understood, told him to take as much time as he needed. He still wasn't sure if that had been a good idea, if his absence wouldn't look like an admission of guilt. Maybe he'd have been better to brave it out, to drag himself into the school and ignore the students' whispers. Maybe he should've stood before them and told them he knew they'd heard what had happened, that it was being dealt with and they should all put it behind them. But was it being dealt with – and how? He had Sarah Dunne on the phone three times a day pleading with him, asking him to take responsibility. He wished she'd never talked him into trying to help the kid.

Patrick Dunne had pretty much flown below Aiden's radar until the accident. A quiet, moody teenager, he wasn't exactly unique at the school. He should've scraped by in the third year exams, but instead he got six honours – the second highest result in the school. He could hold his own in any argument, but refused to join the debating society that Aiden chaired. As far as he could see the boy had only one friend, and that was an enigma. He feared it was more a master-slave situation than a friendship.

The first time he met Sarah Dunne was at the parent-teacher meeting in February. Dressed in a white suit, make-up only on her clear green eyes, she'd worried her short blonde hair and told Aiden she was concerned about her son. Aiden looked at his notes. 'Well his grades are good,' he said. 'Second in the junior cert exams last year.'

Sarah nodded and bit one of her pale pink nails. 'It's not that,' she said. 'It's just he doesn't ... communicate.'

'With you?' Aiden asked.

'With anyone. You must've noticed it at school. I mean, who does he spend his breaks with? Does he talk to the other kids?'

Aiden considered. He'd never really seen Patrick Dunne talking to anyone except Danny Byrne. 'There's one kid, it's an unlikely friendship I'd have thought.'

Sarah Dunne's face had brightened at the mention of a friendship. Aiden wondered just how unsociable Patrick was at home. 'How was Patrick before the accident?'

Sarah straightened and looked away. 'His father's death, you mean? That wasn't an accident. My husband was high, Mr Carty. He locked himself in his car, covered himself in petrol and set himself alight.'

Aiden leaned forward, he had to stop himself from touching her arm. 'I'm sorry. Does Patrick know it wasn't an accident?'

Sarah turned her spectacular green eyes to him. She blinked and swiped a hand under her eye, somehow managing not to disturb the perfect black line around them. She shrugged. 'Patrick was difficult before his father died. Not difficult, maybe that's the wrong word. He's not outwardly uncooperative, it's what he doesn't say that bothers me.'

'Has he seen a counsellor?'

She shook her head. 'No. I mentioned it after his father died, but he said he was fine.'

'I think it'd be a good idea. There's a school counsellor if you don't want to make it too official. Patrick might feel more comfortable.'

Sarah nodded. 'I think he is missing a male influence, was missing it before his father died. He doesn't speak to me, that's for sure. The thing is if it comes from me, this suggestion, he probably won't want to. Do you think maybe you could mention it?'

'Me? Well, I don't really know your son. I've only been teaching him for one term ...'

'But you could try? I like your attitude. I think maybe he'll listen to you.'

She smiled then and Aiden could not refuse her.

When Chloe got home, Aiden's car was already in the drive. He usually got home before her unless he'd something extra-curricular on. Now when she thought about it, he'd been home a lot more in the past few weeks. He must have been helping that boy a lot before whatever had happened happened. She hadn't noticed his absences too much, she was too busy with the musical society. Two weeks before opening night and the actress playing Eva Peron still didn't know her lines, or her lyrics to be more precise. Chloe wondered what time Aiden had turned round and come home that morning. Had he been there all day – doing what? She'd have to tell him she knew. Poor Aiden. Had it been so difficult to tell her?

He was in the shower when she entered the house. His briefcase was in the hall. She listened and then opened the case, it was full of his usual texts and papers. What had she expected? It wasn't like he was masquerading as a teacher. She sighed and eased the clasp closed. A smell of cooking wafted from the kitchen. He'd started dinner. Chloe opened the oven to see what it was. A chicken was browning in its dish, skin wrinkling under the heat.

'Hey, I didn't hear you come in.' Aiden entered the living room wearing a t-shirt and jogging bottoms. His hair was wet. He didn't ask how her day was, but kissed her lightly on the lips. 'Rehearsal tonight?' he asked.

'Yeah, I swear if Amy Watson isn't off book this evening, I'll be tempted to play the part myself.'

Aiden grinned. 'You'd love to, wouldn't you? You're probably hoping she doesn't get it right.'

Chloe shook her head. Aiden brushed past her to look into the oven.

'Aiden, I heard some boys talking on the train this morning.'

'Yeah?' He shut the oven, walked past her without making eye contact.

'Why didn't you tell me?'

'What?' He was hedging, wondering what it was she'd heard.

'About what happened with that Dunne boy. Did he actually hit you?'

'No.' Aiden sat down. 'He headbutted me. Can you imagine? Didn't know what had happened till I was counting stars.'

'Jesus. Why?'

'Why? The kid's not right, Chloe. Who knows his reason for anything?'

'But when did this happen? Why did you not say?'

Aiden put his hands together, elbows on his knees and exhaled. 'Because I was too ashamed. A fifteen-year-old kid laid me flat in the school corridor, and I had to just take it.'

'But he's been expelled, surely?'

He spread his hands. 'Suspended for the moment. There are some who think he should be given another chance, given what happened. They're putting it down to delayed trauma, grief.'

'But why you? You were trying to help him.'

'Again, I don't have an answer. The kid needs proper psychiatric help.'

'What will you do if they take him back?'

'Put in for a transfer maybe. I couldn't stay there, not if

they undermine me like that.'

Chloe crossed the room and put her arms around her husband. 'And that's the thanks you get,' she said. 'For trying to be a good person.'

He wasn't expecting the note. A page torn from a maths copybook lying on the mat inside the front door. It wasn't even in an envelope. Aiden stooped to pick it up, thinking it was something Chloe had dropped on her rush out to rehearsal. 'Come to the house tomorrow at ten. If you don't, Lavelle will be told everything.' Aiden pocketed the note, thankful that Chloe hadn't seen it. Had it simply been luck or had the kid been watching the house and seen her leave. The idea of Patrick Dunne knowing where they lived made Aiden nervous. He had visions of the kid following him home, of him lurking across the street watching the windows, of his eyes following Chloe down the street. There was nothing to stop him telling her everything, or worse – using her as a way of getting at Aiden.

The note instructing him to go to the house. What was that about? And was it coming from the boy or his mother? He cursed himself for his stupidity in getting involved with Sarah Dunne. If he hadn't, none of this would have happened. The lad hadn't cared when he'd caught them together. He'd grinned and said he figured there was a reason Aiden was helping him. It was the closest thing to happy Aiden had ever seen him, but now he understood why – the kid could hold it over him – his affair with his mother. There was no way of ending that without some kind of fallout. He'd figured on it being verbal though, something he could deny. Denial was the only tool he could use – that and the kid's mental state. He relied on Sarah having more tact than having her private business broadcast around her son's school.

A week passed after he'd ended the affair. The kid

didn't show any signs of knowing. Sarah Dunne had tried calling him. He'd taken the call but when she suggested meeting to talk about it, he declined. 'Look Sarah,' he'd said. 'You're lovely, but I should never have let things go as far as they did.'

'And what about Patrick?' she'd said. 'He's so much better with you around.'

This angered him. He wasn't about to let her use the kid to make him feel guilty. 'There's not a lot I can do about that. Maybe he'd agree to see the school counsellor. I should've insisted on it in the first place. I'm sorry, Sarah, but you know my situation. I like you, but the longer we let it continue, the worse for everyone. You must see that.'

And he thought she had seen it. Apart from that phone call and then a text to say she was sorry it had ended, he hadn't heard from her. It was only after the incident, after she was called up to the school and told what her son had done that she pleaded with Aiden to take responsibility. 'I'm not expecting you to tell them the truth,' she'd said. 'If you could accept the blame, say you'd said something to provoke him, that it's your fault. I can't have him kicked out of school, Aiden. What will happen to him?'

Aiden hadn't taken responsibility. Instead, he'd said the kid had huge psychological issues – that he'd attacked him with no good reason, that he was a danger to those around him. He wasn't lying. He believed every word he said. Every conversation he'd had with the boy, he gleaned something disturbing in his manner. When he tried to talk to him about the father's death, he'd shrugged and said it was better with him not around. It was when he'd asked what his mother was like in bed that Aiden started to feel really uncomfortable. The boy wasn't close to his mother, he barely communicated with her, but sometimes Aiden saw him looking at her in a way that wasn't right for a son. He hadn't said it to Sarah. He didn't want to anger – or worse – frighten her. She was convinced that his talks with

Aiden were helping, that his behaviour had improved, but Aiden had serious doubts. And now the note, he couldn't ignore it. Who knew what the kid might do? He was only amazed that the truth hadn't yet come out. It made Aiden anxious that he was saving it up for some grand finale that would result in him losing his job.

'Jesus, Amy. We're less than two weeks from opening night. Can you not get it right?'

Chloe stood, her chair clattered to the floor, the sound echoing round the near-empty hall. She didn't care if she sounded dramatic, she was right. At this rate every person in the theatre would know the lyrics except the actress.

Amy mumbled she was sorry. That she'd get it. During casting, she'd told Chloe that she'd played the part two years before, all she had to do was revise the lines. And she did look the part. Chloe took a deep breath. 'Ok,' she said. 'Let's try that again. From the top.'

Chloe sat back, eyes on the stage. She hadn't meant to lose it with Amy, even if she did deserve it. She wasn't that kind of director. She believed in getting the best from the actors through encouragement, not balling them out in front of the rest of the cast. It was the note that was bothering her. She'd found it on the mat inside the front door just as she was leaving. She picked it up thinking it was a flyer, ready to crumple it up for the bin, and then she'd read it. She was about to take it into the living room to give it to Aiden, but then she stopped. What did the kid mean, Lavelle would be told everything? What was it that Aiden hadn't told her? Chloe had folded the note, put it back where she'd found it and hurried out the door.

Amy stayed back when the others had left. 'Listen Chloe, I'm really sorry. I know I've been messing up at rehearsals. I've a lot going on at the moment. Jimmy's not happy about me taking the part. He thinks I should've waited until Jasmine's a bit older.'

Chloe sighed. 'We knew it was a big commitment when you signed up, Amy. I wouldn't have given you the part if I thought you weren't up to it.'

'But I am. I've done it before. I swear Chloe ...'

Chloe nodded. 'Next time just show it to me. I shouldn't have lost it with you in front of the others either, I'm sorry.'

Amy shrugged. 'Yeah, well.'

The note. Chloe couldn't concentrate on anything, but that note. Normally, she'd have sat Amy down, talked to her about her problems with Jimmy.

'Listen, you'd better get on, no point in giving him something else to grumble about,' she said. Amy grabbed her coat, said 'thanks Chlo' and hurried from the hall. When Chloe got home the note was gone, but Aiden said nothing about it.

Aiden hadn't been able to sleep. As reviled as he was by whatever awaited him at the Dunne house, he was anxious to get there; to discover at last what the boy wanted.

When Chloe left for work, he went upstairs to get ready. He put on smart trousers and a shirt, no harm in reminding the lad he was a teacher, someone in a position of power. Someone who could have him expelled if he wanted to. At least that's what he told himself. Maybe he could convince the boy that the decision lay in his hands, that the suspension was only until he, Aiden, decided the boy's fate.

He stood in front of the mirror, soaped his jaw and shaved. He ran the razor meticulously over his skin, no nicks – no slips, today he was in charge. At 9.30am he got in his car, briefcase in hand and drove to the Dunnes' house.

Sarah opened the door in a white satin robe. Disconcerted, he wondered for a moment if it was she who'd sent the note, a final attempt to rekindle the relationship, but there was nothing suggestive about her manner. She stood back and gestured for him to come in.

'Where is he?'

'Upstairs.'

Aiden glanced up the stairs, but there was no sign of the boy.

The woman turned and walked into the living room and he followed. 'Aiden, couldn't you do something about this, if he gets kicked out of school ...'

'Doesn't matter.' They both looked up at the sound of the kid's voice. He strolled into the room. 'I mean, what does it matter?'

'Patrick, think about the future, you're clever, you came out almost top of the year ...'

'If it doesn't matter, then what's this all about?' Aiden was no-nonsense. He wasn't about to pander to the boy, whatever he threatened him with.

'It's about doing the right thing.'

'The right thing by who? What do mean?'

Patrick Dunne strolled around the room, he stopped by the fireplace and picked up a lighter, he tossed it in the air and caught it again.

Sarah looked worried. 'Pat, what did you call Aiden round here for? Just get to the point.'

'The point is,' the kid said, his eyes not leaving Aiden's face. 'You hurt my mother. Nobody should ever do that.'

Sarah raked a hand through her short blonde hair. She glanced at Aiden. 'Come on Patrick, that was nothing, that doesn't matter.'

The kid looked at her, angry. 'Oh yeah, so what was all the crying about? I can hear you mam, the other side of the wall, crying.'

Sarah looked embarrassed.

'And this moron is going to pay for it.' In a surprisingly swift movement, the kid had locked the door, pocketed the key and taken a can of gasoline from behind the sofa. Aiden attempted to get past him to the door, but the kid sloshed the gasoline at his feet, flicked the lighter and held it aloft. Aiden stepped back, eyeing the gasoline on his shoes.

'Sit down,' the kid said, advancing, the small flame still alight. Aiden retreated towards the sofa. Then the kid stopped him. 'Not yet,' he said. He sluiced the sofa, can swinging, and shoved Aiden into it. The foul-smelling liquid seeped into Aiden's trousers. He made to get up. 'You're crazy,' he said. 'You can't get away with this.'

'Patrick, jesus, what's got into you.' Sarah moved, attempted to grab the lighter away from her son, but she slipped on the spillage. 'Get back,' he barked.

She began to cry. 'Patrick, please.'

The boy started to laugh. 'What, you think Dad's death was an accident?' he said. 'That fucker deserved exactly what he got.'

'Stop. You don't know what you're saying, Pat. And Aiden, Aiden tried to help you.'

For a moment, the kid took his finger from the lighter and the flame went out. Aiden, waiting for his opportunity, leaped from the sofa and slammed into the kid, knocking him to the floor. The lighter flew from his hand and lay there in the gasoline.

Chloe had phoned in sick. She'd told Aiden she was taking the car because she'd to go to her sister's after work. She drove to the end of the road and pulled in at the entrance to the park. There she had a view of the house, but the car couldn't be seen from the road.

When she saw Aiden get into his car, she started the engine and followed, making sure there were at least two cars between them. When Aiden turned into the estate, she slowed. When he pulled up, she stopped at a distance. She didn't see who opened the door, but he disappeared inside the house. 'What now?' she thought. She waited five minutes, but her husband didn't reappear. Anxious, she got out of the car. She walked up the street, not caring now if Aiden suddenly emerged and saw her. She had to know what was going on.

What Chloe saw when she looked through the window was Aiden rushing the boy and the two of them crashing to the floor. There was a woman too, who was attempting to rise when Chloe started banging on the window and shouting her husband's name. For a moment, the three faces looked towards the glass. Then everything was in motion again. The boy hurled himself across Aiden struggling to reach something. Then the woman threw herself on top of the boy. They continued to tussle as Chloe looked round, then grabbed a garden ornament and hurled it against the glass. Aiden, with the distraction of the woman in the white robe, managed to wriggle from beneath the boy just as the ornament crashed through the window. Without stopping, he grabbed the woman's hand, ran to the window and shouted at Chloe to run. A crowd had gathered now on the pavement. The woman attempted to stop. She pulled against Aiden's hand and screamed something. He tried to drag her with him, but she broke free and ran back inside the house. She had just vanished through the window when the explosion sounded and the room was swallowed in flames. Aiden, falling from the wreckage, screamed for someone to dial 911, but Chloe knew that it was too late for the woman and her son.

WIDOW

Andrew was dead. But not in the way that anyone might have expected. No heart attack had crept up on him, raising him on one elbow in the middle of the night. Not an illness either, something we might have looked back on and saw the warning signs, which he'd chosen to ignore. Nor was his death an accident – not in the traditional sense. Andrew hadn't failed to look left and right, hadn't been knocked clear by an N-plate driver who'd run a red light as he crossed from his local Centra, pack of cigarettes in his hand.

No, Andrew was dead, they said, because a few weeks earlier his landlady had chosen to renovate her garden. She instructed the men from the paving company to cobble-lock the driveway in the exact same fashion as the house directly opposite. Then she hung flower baskets either side of the door – the ultimate nod to her neighbours' good taste. This, and the fact that the gunman who put four bullets in Andrew's chest, leaving him to bleed all over his landlady's new driveway, couldn't tell his left from his right. These were the particulars of Andrew Freyne's death.

It was no mystery why I got the call. No surprise that mine was the last number dialled from Andrew's mobile, not even an hour before the terrible event. But now, with his mother crying down the phone, I wished more than ever that I'd insisted on him rectifying the mistake – or at least telling another lie that would obliterate the first one.

Andrew Freyne was my boss. That was what I told the Garda who made the call. The Garda who must have been standing just feet from Andrew's body – who must have taken the phone from his jacket pocket as he lay in a pool of his own blood on his landlady's new cobble-locking. They were attempting to contact next-of-kin, the Garda told me. 'Why, what's happened?' I said, my mind racing, filling up with possible scenarios, things that could have happened in the forty-five minutes since we'd spoken. 'He's not just my boss. We're friends,' I told the guard, soon as I knew that our boss-employee relationship wouldn't be enough to garner any information about what had happened.

They asked if I could identify the body. That there was little doubt, but it would be better to know for certain before getting in touch with the family, none of whom I'd told them were in Dublin. What would be the point in contacting his sister – in tormenting her for the duration of a three-hour car journey to identify someone who wasn't Andrew? I still had my doubts before I saw him. I couldn't imagine him, could imagine anyone but him, lying there, dead. And all the time I couldn't get his voice out of my head. The many outrageous conversations I'd had with him.

'Oh go on, Julia. If you had to, who would it be?' Andrew leaned back in his swivel chair and tossed his biro in the air.

'No one.' I said. 'I never thought about it.'

'Don't give me that,' he said, leaping from his seat. 'It would be Mansfield, wouldn't it? I hear the way the girls talk about him. Can't say I blame them mind ... if only he'd change those

baggy pants for something a bit more ... flattering. So – you want to hear who I'd choose?'

I gave him my disapproving look. 'Andrew, should you be having this conversation with an employee?'

He laughed and sat on the edge of the desk. 'Probably not, but sure who can hear us? Anyway, you'd need some kind of distraction to get you through the day. I'll bet Mansfield has his. Go on then, guess.'

I shook my head. 'I don't know. Rob Wilson,' I said then, just to annoy him. Rob was the stereotype of the I.T. super-nerd.

'What?! Rob ... freaking ... Wilson. Ah Julia, give me some credit. Mind you, if he lost the bifocals and did something with his hair ...'

This time I picked up the pen and threw it at him. 'You, Mr Freyne, are incorrigible.'

He held his hands up, then leaned in conspiratorially. 'Ok, ok. Matt Caine – hands down.'

I laughed, or choked, I'm not sure which, before instinctively looking out the office window down to the sales department where Matt Caine was sitting at his desk.

'What?' Andrew demanded. 'Look at him. I'm telling you, I wouldn't mind finding those shoes next to the bed.'

I started to laugh. 'Christ,' I said. 'Freyne and Caine. That would be some bloody duo. In fairness, though, Andrew, he's hardly the sharpest tool in the box ...'

'It's not the tool, Julia,' he smirked. 'But what you do with it that matters.'

Andrew had started in the company that Autumn. He'd been poached or headhunted from a major distribution firm, and was earmarked as Mansfield's golden boy, the firm anticipating that he'd quadruple sales. He certainly had more charm than his predecessor: a tyrannical misogynist whose departure was lamented by the grand sum of nil, least of all me. From his first day in the office, Andrew set about getting to know the staff. He'd come out of his mezzanine office and call one of us upstairs where the door would close and the summonsed one would not reappear for a half hour at least. For whatever reason, he saved me till last.

'Tell me about your co-workers,' he said, at that first meeting, as soon as I'd finished outlining exactly what I did.

'What do you want to know?' I asked.

'Who would it give you the greatest pleasure to see fired?'

That wasn't hard. Elaine Byrne immediately sprung to mind, Elaine whose hobby it was to invent vicious rumours, but I wasn't about to say it. If there was one thing I'd learned working in an office, it was to keep your beak shut and get on with it.

Andrew and I hit it off straight away, sharing a wicked humour and a taste for cheesy eighties tunes. I was surprised, and then I wasn't, when he started calling me at home in the evenings. I wasn't really one for the phone, it was far handier to fire off a Facebook message, but Andrew and I could easily chat for two hours when he called. We clicked; that was it. And it wasn't long before we started meeting up outside the office. In fact, I'd paid many visits to his landlady's house in the six months that I'd known him.

'We live in the safest housing estate in the country,' he told me, that first evening I'd driven him home.

'Oh?' I'd said, baffled, I hadn't heard great things about Andrew's neighbourhood.

'One of the biggest criminals in the country lives across the street,' he told me.

'And that makes it safe?'

'Sure. There's a Garda car parked at the top of the road every night. With all these gangland killings going on, they clearly think someone's going to try to have a pop at him.'

I wasn't entirely without concerns about the hierarchical nature of our relationship. Sometimes Andrew's invitations came across as orders. He'd even make jokes about it. One night he called and asked what I was doing – as it happened I wasn't doing much – and he told me he wanted me to call over, that he wanted me to drive him somewhere. We hadn't chatted much in the previous few days and I wondered what was going on with him.

'I met this Belgian at the swimming pool last week,' he told me.

'Oh yeah?' Despite myself, I felt a pang of jealousy. Andrew was good-looking, tall, slim, oily black hair – and though I knew he was gay, I'd maybe stupidly held out some hope that he might fancy me. He'd told me, during one of our epic phone chats, that he used to date girls – that he hadn't even known he was gay until he'd stayed in his ex's house and the parents, staunch Catholics, had insisted that he share with her brother. 'Well, one thing led to the other, you see,' he told me at the time. 'And I haven't looked at a girl since, the very idea now, ugh, it makes me sick ...'

'Yeah, yeah,' I'd said. 'I think you've made your point, Andrew.'

The Belgian, he said, was all muscle. He'd visited the house when the landlady was out, and by God that woman's hair would turn white if she knew the things the two of them had got up to. He told me this with a chuckle, one arm out the window as he pulled on a cigarette and we hurtled down the M50.

'It might help if you told me where we're going?' I said, whizzing past yet another exit.

'You know the viewing point at the back of the airport.'

'What? Are we suddenly into planes?' I scoffed.

He blew smoke out, and grinned. 'Well, I do like to get high the odd time,' he said.

It turned out he wasn't joking. He instructed me to pull in at the viewing point. There were three other cars there and Andrew got out and walked up to a dark coloured saloon. When he opened the door, the light went on and I glimpsed a rough looking customer in the driver's seat. Andrew got in, shut the door and the light went off, plunging car and both its occupants into darkness.

'Fuck sake,' I whispered. This wasn't my scene at all – and I hoped that whatever it was he was getting, he'd do it in a hurry, so that we could get out of there.

'Told Clement I'd get him some of this,' he said, waving a small bag under my nose, as he settled back in the passenger seat.

'Does Clement not know any dealers of his own?' I said, a bit too sharply, not liking the position he'd put me in.

'Oh come on, you're not going to turn all Holy Mary on me, are you? It's only a bit of pot.'

'You could've told me where we were going, Andrew. That wasn't exactly fair, was it?'

'Ah, lighten up. Here, let me roll you one. Might loosen you up a bit. Jeez, is it any wonder you're single,' he said. 'Wondered why a good-looking girl like you couldn't bag a bloke – all that mascara makes you look like a fag-hag, but that aside ...'

'If the cap fits,' I shot back.

'Touché,' he grinned, pocketing the pot. I was just glad he didn't light up in the car.

Andrew hailed from Westport, County Mayo, but he'd been in Dublin since he was eighteen when he'd come up to study at Trinity, and he didn't go home much. He said he didn't fit in at home, that they were very conservative. 'My sister didn't even live with her husband before she got married,' he told me. 'Mind you, it worked out, she's three little ones now.' He had a brother too, the complete opposite of him, but a replica of his father who was in the building trade. Turned out it wasn't too long before I was to meet them.

A party was organised to celebrate Andrew's grandmother's ninetieth birthday. 'Do you fancy it?' he asked me. Then more imploringly. 'You'd be saving me from an awful fate going on my own. At least if you were there, it would be a distraction.'

'Why don't you bring Clement?' I asked.

'Oh, come on. We're hardly at that stage,' he said.

'But we are?'

'Now, now, Julia, no need to fish. You know you're my best girl,' he said.

I wasn't sure about the party. Despite hanging out together all the time, there was still the boss thing, and I wondered how the others at work would react if they ever got wind of the fact that I'd been away for a weekend with Andrew. But then, there was no love lost between me and the others in the department, and Andrew said it wasn't any of their business. Besides, who were they going to hear it from anyway, not him. And that being settled, I agreed.

'Great,' he said. 'We'll stay with my sister. You'll love Dee, she's some craic!'

We were driving along, windows down, singing cheesy power ballads at the tops of our voices just before he confessed. 'Jules, look I have to tell you ... they think you're my girlfriend.'

'What? Jesus, Andrew, what did you tell them that for?'

'I didn't, they just assumed, and I didn't contradict them. Do you mind? I mean it's only for one day ...'

'They don't know you're gay?'

'No. My parents are staunch mass-goers. Old school, they'd never understand. I have a cousin that came out and the family disowned him.'

'Are you serious? Wow.' I couldn't make up my mind whether to be annoyed with him for the predicament he'd put me in or feel sorry for him for his reasons.

'So, could you go along with it? Just for today. After a few weeks I can tell them you dumped me, callous bitch that you are.' He winked at me and grinned.

The party took place in a hotel in Westport in the kind of room I'd been in dozens of times at friends' twenty-first birthday parties back in the day, occasions that I always found mildly depressing, but never more so than the gloominess of a pub in the afternoon.

Andrew grabbed my hand just as we reached the function room door and I tried to pull away, but he squeezed my flesh and ignoring my protests raised a hand to greet a girl coming towards us with a baby in her arms.

'Dee, would you look at you. Thin as a whip! This is Julia. She's been dying to meet you. Jules, sweetie, this is Dee. You'd never think she'd just had a baby, would you?'

All this was said in a single breath as Dee smiled and shifted the baby to kiss my cheek. 'He's told us all about you. And I can see he wasn't lying either,' she said, eyes appraising me.

'Oh, I'm sure there was more than one fib thrown in,' I said, and Andrew's fingers tightened on mine.

For the rest of the afternoon babies were thrown into my arms. His sister fussed over me. He was right about Dee, she was some craic. They'd have passed for twins only he was two years younger. She was Andrew in drag with the same broad smile and quick humour. Where his dark curls were shorn close to his head, Dee's hung loose about her shoulders, and the baby clutched at it, mesmerised, as we talked.

It was true that Dee hadn't lived with her husband before they'd married. Her parents would have had a conniption, she said. No one did that in their small community. 'Don't worry,' she said, leaning in conspiratorially, 'I haven't segregated you and Andrew. You know, I used to think ... ach, never mind ... well, I used to think that maybe he was gay,' she said, bouncing the baby on her knee.

'Oh,' I said.

'Well, I wouldn't worry. He's clearly not, not from what I hear. I hear you two are ... well, I hear you can't get enough of one another. It's just he never went out with girls back home. Not when he went up to Dublin either. At least he never brought any back here. And then the whole thing with what happened at the seminary.'

'The seminary?'

Dee looked at me, wide-eyed. 'Oh Christ, you didn't know?'

I shook my head. Lost as to what might be the correct answer to this particular curve-ball.

'Andrew went to Maynooth, he was training to be a priest, but he dropped out in the final year. Didn't he tell you?'

'We haven't known each other that long.' I floundered.

'What did you think?'

I shrugged, not wanting to make Andrew out to be a liar. 'I just assumed he'd studied marketing,' I said.

'Yeah, but that was after. Look, don't let on I told you, will you?' she said. 'He'll have my guts ... you probably know how moody he can be. Don't get me wrong, he's great, it's just you have watch your Ps and Qs with him sometimes ... Anyway, we're glad he's met someone. You'll just have to keep him in line, that's all. And I'm sure you're well able for that.'

Andrew looked over at that moment and blew me a kiss. He was enjoying this, the bastard. And I could have killed him for embroiling me in his deceit.

True to her promise, Dee had put Andrew and me in her spare bedroom.

'Which side do you sleep?' he asked, smirking and throwing himself down on the left-hand side of the bed.

'That side,' I said. 'Not that it's going to matter much because you'll be crashing on the couch.'

'What? And have them think we've fallen out already?' he said.

'Yes, why not? That way it won't come as a surprise when you tell them I've dumped you.'

He patted the mattress and gave me his come-to-bed eyes. 'They'd be heartbroken,' he said. 'Dee loves you. And besides, I've already told her we're at it like dogs in heat. They'd never believe you'd thrown me out.'

'Jesus, Andrew. Don't you feel bad about this?'

'What?'

'The lies.'

He shook his head. 'If they weren't so bigoted, I wouldn't have to, would I? It's their doing. Otherwise, I'd be here with Clement.'

An hour later, lying in the dark next to him, I was still awake.

'How come you never told me about the seminary?' I said.

Andrew shifted in the small double bed, his leg brushing mine, and I pulled back so that I was right on the edge.

'Jeez, Dee told you that?'

'She thought I knew. She actually said that she'd thought you were gay when you joined the seminary. Could you not tell her? You seem to get on so well ...'

'Dee's great – we're very close, but believe it or not, she's just as bad as the rest of them when it comes to that.

And she'd never keep it to herself, it'd be on the crossroads.'

'What happened at the seminary?'

He laughed. 'What? Did I get thrown out for shagging one of the other recruits? I wish I had! No, I just decided it wasn't for me. My mother wanted it more than I did – proud as punch, she was. It nearly killed her having to tell her friends I'd left. Thought I'd take after uncle Gerry. One of those in the family was enough.'

'Your uncle's a priest?'

'He was. Had a heart attack while buggering an altar boy round the back of the sacristy.'

'You're kidding ...'

The mattress shook with Andrew's laughter. 'Couldn't resist the cliché. He did have a heart attack though. Poor Gerry. Now he can't even have a pint – that along with no sex, I can't think what his *raison d'etre* might be.'

When Andrew called me up to the office on Monday, he was on the phone. He indicated for me to close the door so the staff in the office below couldn't hear. 'Hang on a second, Julia's here, she wants to tell you how much she enjoyed the party.' I mouthed no to the receiver that was thrust into my hand. It was his mother, saying she hoped it wouldn't be long before we made it out west again. Bile rose in my throat. 'One day, Andrew. That was the agreement. You needn't expect me to go along with this indefinitely.'

'Oh, go on. Don't pretend you didn't enjoy it,' he said. 'Me, you, that double bed. Sure aren't you half in love with me already?' He turned serious then. 'You do know though that there's no chance, don't you? I'm gay, not bi. Just so we're clear on that.'

When I saw Andrew's body in the morgue, I was tempted to say it wasn't him because it wasn't really.

Andrew could never be that still. I expected him to sit up and make some sarcastic remark.

I went into his Facebook account and looked up his friends. I ought to tell Clement, I thought, but I didn't. Dee took control of everything. She and her husband insisted that I be included in the funeral arrangements despite my protests that Andrew and I had only been together a little while and that it wouldn't seem right. 'Nonsense,' she said. 'He was mad about you.'

In the funeral home we leafed through the catalogue of coffins. I surprised myself by insisting on a white one with brass handles. I'd intended going along with everything Dee suggested, but I knew Andrew would have loved this charade. It was only when the undertaker came to the death notice that I panicked. 'Sadly missed by his beloved partner Julia.' Dee suggested, making it sound as though Andrew and I had spent a lifetime together.

'No, it wouldn't be right,' I told her. My mind reeled trying to find an excuse as to why I shouldn't be named, and then I landed on it.

'Of course it would, you were crazy about each other,' she said.

I nodded. I was crazy about Andrew, I had been from the moment we met, but this was my chance to put an end to this charade.

'Could we have a minute?' I asked the funeral director. He stood respectfully and went into the next room, where Andrew's body would be laid out the following day, and closed the door softly behind him. Dee and I were alone in that office with death all around us.

'Sorry Dee, but I have to tell you something ... my name can't appear in that notice.'

She took my hand and squeezed it. 'Go on.'

'The staff at work ... they didn't know about us. We preferred to keep it private – they're awful gossips and it would have made things very awkward, Andrew being my boss ...'

Brava, Jules, I heard Andrew say. And Dee looked so much like him in that moment that I almost expected her to smirk and tell me she knew everything, that she'd known all along, but she didn't. Instead, she squeezed my hand and told me she understood.

The only one to travel to Westport for the funeral was Mansfield. If he was surprised to see me among the mourners in the front pew of the church, he didn't show it. He shook my hand with all the others, and after the service I saw him get into his Mercedes to make the trip back to Dublin.

Soup and sandwiches were served in the same hotel Andrew and I had been to only a fortnight before at his grandmother's party. His extended family greeted me as though I were the grieving widow, and all the time Andrew's voice in my head. *Brava Jules.* And I felt it in the gut, his loss, as any widow would.

The Dare

Gary was the one who'd spotted the number. They'd spilled from the train, crossed over the footbridge and descended to the platform; an ungainly gaggle of fifth years, exuberant that they'd made it to the mid-term break. It was on one of those sticky notes, illuminous pink, and in a spidery black hand it read *Debra*.

Gary stooped and picked up the paper. 'Hey Julian, have you lost your girlfriend's number?'

Julian leaned in to examine the note, then swiped it from his fingers. 'Whihoo. A number at last!' he said, holding the pink paper aloft as he pirouetted down the platform. The rest of the lads laughed and he stopped prancing to pass it round. 'Like in the song,' Danny said. 'What?' 'You know ... her name was Deb-o-rah ...' he sang, but he didn't get a chance to continue as a hand was clamped over his mouth.

'Somebody should ring it,' Julian said. 'Gary – you're the one that found it.'

Gary shook his head. 'Go on, triple dare you,' the shout went up. Gary looked at the note. Debra – nice name. Not spelt in the usual way either. Maybe she was one of those Italian girls studying at the language school on the seafront – dark wavy hair, and tanned legs showing under cropped jeans.

'Ok, ok,' he said. He took out his phone, tapped in the number. The lads hung around outside the station waiting while the phone buzzed in Gary's left ear. 'Yeeaaaaaah?' The voice was muffled, sounded like the speaker had been woken. 'Hello, is that Debra?' Gary said, not having a clue what he was going to say next. There was a silence, then some unintelligible sound, yawning maybe. 'Who the hell wants to know?' she said. Gary hung up. Whoever Debra was, she didn't sound like she'd appreciate a crank call.

'What? What happened?' one of the lads asked.

'Nothing.'

'What do you mean nothing? What did she say?'

'It wasn't her.' Gary stuck the post-it note in his pocket.

'What do you mean it wasn't her?' Julian asked.

'I don't know. Maybe it was a wrong number.'

Gary was in his room doing homework when his phone rang. 'Who's this?' the voice asked. 'Julian,' he said. He recognized Debra's voice. 'Why did you call me before?' Gary looked at his maths copybook and deciding it would be less complicated, he told the truth. 'It was a dare. We found your number on a sticky note.' 'Where?' the woman asked. 'Bray station.' She breathed heavily into the phone. He wondered if she might be drunk. 'Bray,' she repeated. 'Yeah, Bray.' In the background, Gary could hear a strange noise. It sounded like a dog whining, or maybe it was a television. 'Look, I'm sorry,' he said. 'It was a dumb joke.' The woman didn't answer. After a moment, she spoke again. 'I'm going to kill myself, Julian,' she said. 'You're the last person I'll ever speak to. Isn't that strange? We've never even met.'

Gary had been doodling on his copybook. Now, he

threw down the pen. This was no fifteen-year-old exchange student. This was a woman who needed help. 'Don't do that,' he said. 'Why not?' the woman asked. 'Well, what about your family, your friends?' 'I don't have any friends,' she said. 'Where are you?' Gary asked, picking up the pen again. 'I'll come see you.' 'What? Are you going to be my friend, Julian?' the woman laughed. But it wasn't really a laugh – more a forced cackle. 'If you want,' he said. 'I'd ... I'd like to meet you.' 'Why? Why would you want to meet me?' Gary looked round, trying to think of something to say. 'Because you sound interesting,' he said. 'Mad you mean. Suicidal.' She laughed again. 'Why did you say you called me?' She was definitely drunk. 'For your address,' he said. 'I'm coming to help you.'

Gary stood outside the grey terraced house and put his finger on the bell. The sharp buzz that he expected didn't sound so he couldn't tell if it was working. Instead, he raised the brass knocker and listened to it echo through the eerily quiet house. In the porch, several pot plants wilted; leaves shrivelled by the sun. A no junk mail sign on the letterbox was ignored, its gaping mouth stuffed with fliers. He jumped when he felt something at his legs. When he looked down a small grey cat miaowled up at him. Gary wasn't fond of cats. Not since his grandmother's ginger Tom had sunk its teeth into his arm, and so he eyed this cat sceptically as it butted its small head against him.

Thinking about his grandmother gave Gary an idea. He shooed the cat away and lifted the first pot plant. There was nothing beneath but a brown streak on the lino, where a long time ago, water had run. He turned over each pot until finally the one closest the wall yielded what he'd been hoping to find, a single brass key like the one for his own front door.

Gary stepped into the hall. The house was dark. On the banister a blue raincoat hung, and a pair of mud-caked boots poked from under the stairs. Upstairs, he heard voices. When he stopped by the banisters to listen, he discovered it was a radio talking. 'Hello?' he called. Nobody answered. Cautiously, he climbed the first few steps of the stairs. He almost let out a yelp when something brushed past him and he realised that the cat must have darted in ahead of him when he'd opened the door. 'Hello?' he said again, this time raising his voice. The last thing he wanted to do was to frighten the woman.

Just as he reached the landing there was a thump. 'Debra?' Gary called, the woman's name sounded strange on his lips. There was a groan, followed by the cat's miaowling. 'How did you get in here, huh?' he heard the woman say, but she was talking to the cat who'd jumped onto the bed where she was perched. Gary tapped on the door frame and she looked up, startled. 'What the fuck are you doing in here?' she said, grabbing the bottle from the bedside locker. Gary lifted his hands to protect himself as she flung the bottle, barely missing his head. It crashed against the wall, but didn't smash and rolled along the carpet. 'I'm Julian,' Gary said, as the woman got to her feet and stood there swaying. 'We talked on the phone remember?' 'Julian, Christ you're a child,' she said, and he suddenly felt very self-conscious standing there in his school uniform. The woman sat on the edge of the bed again. She was wearing nothing but a t-shirt and she didn't bother to cover her bare legs.

'You said you were going to kill yourself,' Gary said.

She took a packet of cigarettes from the locker, put one between her lips and groped round for a lighter. 'Yeah, well, decided I couldn't be bothered,' she said. 'You got a light, Julian?' He shook his head. 'Actually, my name's Gary.' The woman laughed. 'I prefer Julian,' she said, the cigarette bobbed between her lips, unlit.

Gary looked round the darkened room. It was a mess. A mountain of clothes piled on a chair had erupted onto the floor and lay strewn across the carpet. He stepped round them and with a swift movement, pulled back the curtains. Debra put a hand to her eyes. 'Jesus, Julian,' she said. He stood by the window, waited until she lowered her hand from her eyes. She looked round, dazed, the cigarette growing soggy in her mouth.

'When did you last eat?' Gary asked. Debra shrugged, kicked at another empty bottle by the bed. 'The doctor says fluids are what's important.' 'Have you seen a doctor?' She laughed, 'Doctors know shit about my problem.' Debra leaned on her hands and pushed herself back against the pillows. She drew her legs up, the t-shirt too short to cover her. Gary looked away. He thought of his mother, how her legs had become bird-like, too thin almost to support her. Debra, in the harsh light, looked about his mother's age. She'd have been fifty on her next birthday. Thinking of her made his eyes sting, and he turned abruptly from the woman.

'I'll make you something to eat,' he said. Debra rubbed the cat's belly as it lay on its back and stretched its paws towards her. The kitchen was surprisingly clean, everything in its place. Unfortunately, all he found in the fridge was an outdated carton of eggs and some sour milk. He closed it again and looked in the cupboards. This time he found a tin of porridge and a carton of condensed milk, which he figured would be better than nothing.

'Jeez Julian, you're well-trained,' the woman said. She'd found a lighter some place and now smoke wafted round the room, curling upwards. Gary watched her poke the porridge with the spoon, the cigarette still in her mouth. 'Why did you want to kill yourself?' he asked. Debra pushed the porridge round, but didn't eat. 'Because it's all gone,' she said. 'Everything. Everyone.' She sounded, suddenly, sober.

'What do you mean?' Gary asked. 'Where did they go?'

'What? Nowhere,' she said. 'They were never here to

begin with.' She waved her cigarette, the bowl slid to the edge of the tray, stopped just short of falling. Gary was beginning to wish he'd never made that call, had never come here to help this strange woman.

'My mother died,' he said. 'She didn't want to. She fought till there was no fight left in her.' Those were his dad's words when he'd tried to console Gary.

Debra took a puff on the cigarette. 'She's lucky,' she said. 'Why would anyone want to hang round this dump?'

Gary felt the anger deep in his stomach. He wanted to take the bowl and fling it, like the woman had done with the bottle, against the wall. Watch the porridge drip down the pink paintwork. What right had she to want to take her own life? 'You don't know what you're talking about,' he said. 'Look at you sprawled here feeling sorry for yourself.'

The woman gave him a look. 'Don't judge me, Julian,' she said.

'It's Gary,' he said.

'Whatever. If you came here looking for another mother, boy did you get the wrong number ...'

'I came here to help,' Gary said, angry with himself for the catch in his voice. This woman could never compare to his mother, but he'd thought maybe he could help, maybe he could save her.

'You should go on your way now, Julian,' the woman said. 'If I see your mother, I'll tell her hello.' She puffed on the cigarette, picked up the empty bottle from the floor and stared at it hard. She continued looking at it until he turned and stomped out of the room.

In anger, Gary pulled the bunch of fliers from the mouth of the letterbox, letting it snap shut. Among them there were letters, half a dozen of them, unopened. He lifted one from the pile. Ms Debra O'Connor, it said. URGENT! Gary glanced up the stairs. There were voices coming from the woman's room again. She'd turned the radio up loud. He stood there, the letters in his hand, and wondered if he ought to go back up and give them to her.

'Debra.' Her head lolled against the pillow; mouth slightly open. Stealthily crossing the room, he placed the bundle of letters on the bedside table. As he did so, a crumpled piece of paper by the bed caught his eye. He cast a glance at the woman before picking it up. In the corner of the letter was the government crest and in bold type: *Department of Social Services.* Three short sentences informed Debra that her appeal for custody of her daughter, Lara O'Connor, had been turned down by the High Court. On the radio, music replaced the voices. The woman stirred, bleary eyes fixing on the paper in his hand. 'Just who do you think you are?' she said, attempting to sit up. 'Who the hell do you think you are?' Gary dropped the letter – the woman's screams following him down the stairs. 'Get the hell out, do you hear me? Get the hell out and don't ever come back here again.'

BAT EARS AND FIFI

The dog had big bat-like ears, his head oversized for his short legs and his long white body. But Fifi knew as soon as he pottered over to the fence, silent, among the barking melee, that this was the one.

At first, she wondered if the GPS had sent her on a wild goose chase. The narrow boreen grew narrower still, hedges scratching at the car windows like bony claws, until finally it opened onto a clearing. Trundling over a cattle grid, and through a wide set of gates, Fifi surveyed the space around her. In a field to the right, a pair of chestnut horses grazed and ahead of her at the end of the dirt track stood a wooden prefab. Coming towards her down the track were two girls, one of them being pulled along by an oversized mongrel, whilst the other walked a young brown boxer. The girl with the boxer raised a hand in greeting as they side-stepped the car and Fifi loosened her fingers from the wheel in response.

Stepping from the car, Fifi attempted to avoid the mud. Her arrival had provoked a cacophony of barking from inside the prefab, the culprit, a Jack Russell peered out at her through a window and she saw a shadow of movement inside. A few minutes later an elderly woman, dressed in men's trousers and boots, opened the door and the Jack Russell came running out. It halted a few feet shy of her yapping excitedly, making her question her being there at all.

'Don't mind Lucy,' the old woman said. 'She's got a mouth on her, but she wouldn't bite.' Bending down, she scooped the dog up in her arms. The barking stopped, but a low growl persisted.

'I'm looking for a dog,' Fifi said.

'Plenty of them here. What are you after?'

'I'm not sure. I'm not fussy about the breed, just nothing too big. I'll know when I see it.'

Fifi followed the woman round the back, past the sign that read *Staff Only* until they came to a yard with dozens of dogs. As soon as they caught sight of the old woman, a bunch of them ran towards the fence, scrambling for attention, one barking and setting the rest of them off.

'Who's this?' Fifi squatted down to be on a par with the bat-eared dog. Cautiously, he put a nose to her palm and then licked it.

'That's Perkins,' the old woman said. 'You want to meet him?'

The days leading up to Perkins home check were the busiest Fifi had known since her mother's passing. She scrubbed the floors, gathered the piles of books scattered round her small house and arranged them in double rows on the shelves already warped by so much weight. She was ruthless in her clearing; anything unnecessary was chucked or put aside for the local charity shop. Things that might be deemed a hazard to her new companion were taped down or sacrificed without a further thought. She got in a local man to reinforce the garden fence with chicken wire. By the time the woman from the shelter came the house was almost as uncluttered as the day she'd bought it.

'Is there someone here during the day?' the woman asked.

Fifi nodded, thought about her brother and how he said it was unhealthy all the time she spent alone in that house. And it did get lonely, she wouldn't deny that. Weekends were the worst – on a Friday evening facing into another weekend she was almost tempted to lift the phone and call someone, but who? So, instead, she'd go online and read the news. She'd read all the comments on a thread of angry people until she could feel her own blood rise. 'I don't know why you bother ...' Mark used to tell her. 'Why do you let things get to you the way you do?' Because I care, she thought. Because I care more than other people do.

And that was the reason she'd quit her job to care full-time for her mother. The reason why things had come to an end with Mark. Though that had been his choice not hers. 'I don't see your brother making these sacrifices. Surely, your mother can manage on her own for a bit?' he'd said. 'Surely, she doesn't need you racing over there every other minute?'

Even then she hadn't seen it coming. It was only when she was leaving his house one Sunday afternoon that he'd said she may as well take her things with her because who knew when she'd make it over again. 'What do you mean?' she said. She'd always left a bag there with clean clothes – she liked the idea of her things in his place. 'I don't mean anything. It's just – it seems like your mother needs you more right now, that's all.'

After that his calls became more infrequent. Weekends, the time they always spent together, the time when her brother, to give him his dues, took their mother out and kept her overnight in his place, Mark took to going on fishing trips with his brother. 'I'm sorry,' he told her, as he announced his absence yet again. 'But he's going through a bit of a rough patch. I could bring you out on Wednesday night instead?' Wednesdays she had to bring and collect her mother from her dialysis appointment. He knew it was weekends or nothing for her these days. And so what little time they spent together was whittled down to nothing. But it didn't stop the hurt when it came.

'It's very cosy,' the woman from the shelter said. 'And the garden, is it secure? You know there have been a lot of problems with dog theft lately, but I expect you'd keep him indoors?'

Fifi assured her that she would; she pointed out the place where she envisioned putting his little bed. The woman smiled and told her she could see that she really wanted him. That it would just take a few days to sort out the paperwork. He'd be microchipped and given his shots and then Perkins – Mr Perkins – as she'd decided to call him, would be hers.

That very same afternoon, Fifi drove to the pet superstore. She bought two matching bowls, one for food and one for water with a pattern of little white bones on the black enamel. Next, she investigated the beds, was about to pick up a sensible canvas affair that could be wiped clean when she spotted a tartan one instead. By the time she got to the counter, she'd accumulated an array of squeaky toys, chew toys, tennis balls, tug ropes, and, most importantly, a medal, on which she asked the girl in the store to engrave his name and her phone number.

Mr Perkins' arrival changed things. That first night she brought his bed into her bedroom so that he wouldn't be lonely. The next morning she woke when she felt a soft thud at the end of the bed and opened her eyes to find him standing there looking at her expectantly. He was a young dog, only about five months the old woman had told her, and Fifi soon found her empty days filled with walks, throwing things and any other activity she could think of to keep her new companion entertained.

It had been only a year since Fifi's mother died. That first year she'd been plagued with nightmares. She'd dream of her mother sick, of her mother dying and telling her that she didn't want to go without her. Those first nights, spent in her mother's house alone, it had taken hours for sleep to come. Fifi wasn't beyond superstition and in the dark, she'd wonder if her mother would come to take her. When her brother suggested selling the house, it had come as a relief. There was too much of her old life here, of her old self. A new start was what she needed. And so as soon as the house was sold – and she was temporarily living with her brother, she began scouring the internet for a home to match her budget.

Her brother and sister-in-law had urged her not to rush into anything, offering assurances that she could stay as long as she wanted, but when she came across the cottage, she'd seized the opportunity. It was the location that was the real clincher; right on the wild Atlantic way. 'What will you do there? You don't know anyone,' her brother had said. But if there was one thing that the break-up with Mark had taught her, it was that she could survive alone. And this place with its vast open spaces, its rugged cliffs and wild sea was exactly what she needed to heal.

The first few months had been a challenge. Particularly when out of curiosity one evening she'd looked up Mark on Facebook to see that not only had his girlfriend, the one who'd appeared on the scene an indecently short time after he'd finished it with her, moved in with him, but that they'd since acquired a three-year-old son and by the looks of his girlfriend's rounded stomach, had another one on the way. It was five years since the break-up. And sometimes, in her head, she thanked him for it. She knew that as difficult as it had been losing her mother, it would have been much worse if her heart hadn't already been broken.

Her brother was dead against the move. 'What are you going to do out there? It won't be good for your mental health. You need to get back to work – to some semblance of normality,' he'd told her. 'What – like you?' she said, though she hadn't meant to be unkind. Her brother had a decent job, but the fact was he spent every hour of every day doing it.

Fifi had a plan, but it wasn't one she wanted to share with anyone. The money she'd inherited from her mother would be enough to tide her over for at least the next two years. She might teach some classes to top it up, but then again she might not. Instead, she'd paint. She'd paint the cliffs, and the wild sea. She'd paint Mr Perkins if she could get him to sit long enough. She hadn't earned a degree in fine art to spend eight hours a day in an office. No – when she quit her job, she knew that she'd never go back to that.

Mr Perkins settled in just fine. He'd whine outside the bathroom door when she went to the toilet, and she considered leaving the door ajar, but it would have been pure strange to have a male of any description watching her as she squatted on the seat. And so instead she'd talk to him through the closed door. The sound of her own voice almost startled her these days. She'd been six months in the cottage and the only neighbour whose name she knew was the man who'd fixed the fence.

In the beginning, she kept Mr Perkins on a leash, afraid that in his enthusiasm, he might run right off the cliff, but the dog was cautious and applied the brakes as soon as they got close enough to gaze down on the rocks. She didn't realise that just as he'd got used to gambolling free along the cliffs, she would have to return him to his leash for reasons that were not his fault.

The marks appeared on the gate pillar overnight. Or it could have been early morning. Either way, she hadn't seen them until they'd come back from their first walk down to the beach. She'd read all the signs on a Facebook forum: zip ties on garden gates, chalk marks on the pavement, white vans cruising down private roads where they had no business going. She stopped to examine them: two parallel black lines. She ushered Mr Perkins inside and locked the door behind them.

All that morning she found herself going to the windows. She drove into town to the local hardware and bought a tin of white paint, taking Mr Perkins with her. When they got back, she set about covering the marks, which she'd tried to wash off, but they appeared to have been made in indelible marker.

Mr Perkins sat up in the window watching. She knew he'd be whining to join her, but she'd take no chances. As she was finishing up, she spotted a white van on the road, but it passed swiftly, the driver not so much as turning his head to look at the house. As she straightened and gathered up the paint tin and cloths, she wondered if fresh paint were an even bigger signal – a white flag in enemy territory.

The updates on the forum began to saturate her feed: a liver and white springer spaniel had gone missing a couple of miles away; the suspects were a woman and a man spotted in a four by four with a yellow registration; an update on a pair of golden cockers which had been stolen two months before reported that one of the dogs had been recovered in the UK, the microchip cut from the animal. Another comment said that dogs were being smuggled through the port; Gardaí in Dublin had seized a litter of pups in the back of a van on its way to the ferry and the driver had failed to produce papers. Fifi shuddered and swore an oath to keep Mr Perkins close to her.

In the local DIY store, she bought a padlock for the garden gate and two halogen sensor lights. She installed one above the front door and the other at the back of the house. That way, she'd be alerted if anyone dared to breach the fence and came within five metres of her door. She took to putting the dog on his lead when she let him out last thing at night for fear that anyone was lurking round the property.

Mr Perkins, unaware of his mistress's fears, continued to thrive. A lively animal, Fifi could never get him to sit still long enough to paint, so she began taking pictures to work from. On impulse, she sent one of these pictures to her brother on WhatsApp with a brief note that said "A new friend." Her brother wrote back to say would she not have got a bigger dog, something that could protect her? She switched off the phone and wondered why she'd bothered.

She was in bed that night when the halogen light at the back of the house clicked on and Mr Perkins began kicking up a racket. She turned on the bedside lamp, and tried to calm him, but the dog ran to the window and continued to bark, hair bristling. She grabbed the bat she kept next to the bed, a solid piece of wood her father had always kept hanging from a nail on the wall in case of intruders, and crept to the window. She was relieved when she lifted the curtain to see a fox moving stealthily round the yard, the last thing on view a bushy tail as he disappeared round the corner of the shed. She laughed to herself and put the bat back by the bedside and heard her father's voice. *God help anyone who comes in here. They'll not get out the same way.*

The next morning when she went out to remove the padlock from the gate, it was gone. The gate was still closed and looking round it didn't seem as though anything had been disturbed, but its absence unsettled her. She thought back to the evening before. Could it be that she'd forgotten to put the lock on, that she'd got distracted and put it down somewhere? She honestly couldn't say. She searched the house for the missing lock and could only conclude that someone had taken it in the night.

Her fears were vindicated by the arrival of the postman.

'You'd want to keep everything locked up,' he told her, as he handed her the morning's mail. 'The Clearys were robbed last night. Two bikes stolen from the garden shed. They attempted to take the ride-on mower too, had it halfway down the garden when something must've disturbed them.' Fifi didn't know who the Clearys were, but she figured they must be the neighbours a field away. The woman often waved to her as she drove past. 'So, it wasn't you they were coming for after all. It was you scared them away,' she told Mr Perkins, rubbing his ears, as she watched the postman's van vanish at the turn of the road. 'Nothing worth robbing in our shed anyway,' she said. All that was out there was a lawnmower that stunk of petrol left behind by the previous owner. If someone stole that, they'd only be doing her a favour.

That evening when she brought Mr Perkins out in the yard, she took a flashlight and her father's bat with her. If anyone came at them in the dark, she wouldn't think twice about using it. The dog snuffled round the grass, as he always did, looking for just the right place to go. It was a clear night and Fifi stood admiring the stars. She'd been standing a few minutes, eyes trained on the sky, when it came to her attention that Mr Perkins was eating something. She jerked the lead, shouting: *drop it. Drop it.* But the dog turned this way and that as she tried to wrestle whatever was in his mouth away from him. When he did finally drop a piece and she snatched it away, she found it was a lump of meat, which she fired as far as she could over the fence. 'Naughty. Naughty boy,' she said, already worrying that someone might have flung the meat into the garden.

Mr Perkins was sick that night. She woke to hear a strange rumbling sound and saw him standing by the bed heaving. The undigested lump of meat came back up and she grabbed it before he could eat it again and mopped up the bile that had accompanied it. When she got back into bed, he came with her. The small warm heft of his body pressed against her and he laid his head on her shoulder. 'You're alright.' she said. 'You'll be alright.' And she lay there awake, not willing to disturb him, as his breath deepened in sleep.

The next morning, he was well again. Tail wagging as he skipped round her in the kitchen.

Her Facebook feed was full of notifications again. She'd told herself to stop reading them – all they did was fuel her anxiety, but she couldn't help but skim through.

J.P: *Caught a man trying to lure my two dogs with meat at the garden gate. Was leaning in to grab the smaller one when I ran out of the house.*

Rob: *Why the hell are people leaving their dogs outside when this is going on? Please keep your dogs in the house!*

J.P: *My dog is kept inside dick head. But he's a dog, he's to go to out for obvious reasons I suppose you'll suggest potty training next?!*

Fifi scrolled through some of the other updates. A couple of lost dogs believed to have been stolen had turned up safe. Apparently, they'd got stuck in a neighbour's shed and stayed there for two days until the homeowners had come back after a weekend away. More reports of zip ties on wheelie bins, white vans cruising down cul de sacs, yellow registration plates. Someone had posted about couriers coaxing dogs into the backs of their vans when making deliveries. Even postmen were coming under fire accused of being in cahoots with the thieves. Paranoia was rife and ultimately powered by these posts. She ought to leave the group, she thought. But then wasn't it always better to be informed?

The next morning before she took Mr Perkins outside, Fifi walked round the garden checking that there was no more of the meat that had made him sick. She was skirting the inside of the fence when she stopped and stared at a print on the ground. The patterned sole of a runner moulded in the mud. Only one, but the grass had been flattened by the weight of another. She stooped down to examine it. The ridges, still limber from last night's rain, flattened easily beneath her finger. Fresh prints, but not hers.

Fifi checked the padlock on the gate. Not much use when intruders could still jump the fence. She'd have to call that man again, the one who'd reinforced it with chicken wire, and see if he could add to the existing fence to make it higher. She'd buy a post box too – that way she wouldn't have to take the lock off for the postman in the mornings. He could simply slip the post in from outside the gate. The bars were just about wide enough.

Fifi took another trip to the DIY store. This time she bought bolts – one for the front door and one for the back. Then as an after-thought, she bought another for the bedroom. That way if someone managed to force their way into the house, she and Mr Perkins could lock themselves in the room while she called for help. Next, she went outside to the garden area. Where normally, she loved to browse the flowers, today she strode directly to an assistant to ask if there was anything she could buy to keep people from getting over her fence.

'We've got rolls of barbed wire,' the young man told her. 'Or razor wire if you really want to keep people out. How long a fence are we talking about?'

Fifi told him the measurements and the assistant offered to wheel the cart with the two rolls of wire out to the car. As they were crossing the car park, Fifi saw a man looking in the window of her car. She always left it open an inch for Mr Perkins and this man seemed to be mouthing something through the gap in the glass. From where they were, she couldn't see Mr Perkins in the back seat. She began to walk faster – the assistant attempting to keep up with the cart. 'Hey,' she said. 'What are you doing there?' But the man, already walking away, paid her no notice. He zapped his key, unlocking the doors of a white van, and got in and drove away.

'You ok?' the assistant asked, as she opened the boot – her eyes tracking the van as it pulled out of the carpark. Mr Perkins growled a welcome, ran up and down the back seat as the assistant loaded the roles of wire into the boot. 'Nice dog,' he said, reaching in to pat him. 'No!' she said, a little too forcefully, gripping the assistant's arm. 'It's just he might bite.'

'Probably no need to build up the fence once you've this stuff,' the man said, as he stood surveying the roles of wire. 'Is it him you're trying to keep in, or other folk out?' He laughed and nodded to Mr Perkins who was perched on the window ledge looking out.

It took the man all that afternoon and the next to roll the wire right round the fence. The coils stood a foot high over the wooden stakes giving the impression of a high security prison or a concentration camp. Fifi locked the gate after the man had gone and allowed Mr Perkins the run of the yard. 'No one's going to get through that,' she said, as she flung the ball and watched the dog race after it, ears flying, before he brought it back and dropped it at her feet.

When Fifi looked in the fridge that evening, she discovered stocks were low. Damn it. She'd meant to go to the supermarket, but the man in the carpark had unnerved her and she didn't want to leave Mr Perkins in the car alone after that.

'Want to share?' she said, looking at her companion digging into his bowl of kibble. He wagged his tail and continued to eat. Fifi took a packet of fish fingers from the freezer – opened the last can of beans and emptied it into a pot. Then she had an idea: she could order her groceries from the supermarket online. They could deliver and there'd be no need for her to leave the house. No need to leave Mr Perkins alone.

Fifi clicked into Facebook. There were several new notifications in the group. A dog had gone missing in Clare; the owner was offering a substantial reward. Another that had been reported missing several months before had potentially been spotted for sale on a website. Once flagged, the ad had been removed, but not before someone had taken and posted a screenshot. Fifi sighed and closed the browser. There was only so much she could take. Mr Perkins moved closer to her on the sofa and she ran her fingers through his soft fur and lowered her face to his muzzle. 'We're safe now,' she muttered. 'No one can get to us in here.' The bat-eared dog turned intelligent eyes up to hers and licked her face, ever-trusting.

DISCLOSURE

'Is it ok for you?' The hairdresser, attractive but for the tattoos twisted round his arms, holds the mirror to the back of her head. She nods. 'Great,' she says. 'It's perfect.' She can barely look at herself. She turns her head from side to side, eyes cast slightly beyond the glass. They flit to and from the dazzling print of the black and white wallpaper, unable to settle on her reflection.

'That's fifty euros,' he says. He smiles at her in a way that she's only seen men smile at Riona.

Outside, she pulls the collar of her coat up. She's not used to the breeze on her skin. Several times, she lifts her hand to feel the hair tapered at the back of her neck, and almost expects the red dye to have stained her fingers. She likes how it feels, but it's raw: the feeling. It will be raw, she's been told, for many months to come.

In a department store, she stands baffled by the number of cosmetic counters. These counters are manned by girls in white coats, some with heavy make-up, red lips and smoky eyes. Others are pale-skinned, nude-lipped. They eye their prey; the ones who look undecided, certain to be an easy sell. She sees that one of them has homed in on her and prepares to submit. She's a plump girl with flawless skin, a sheen on her cheeks, and a perfectly contoured jaw. Her eyes are dark like a gypsy's. She steps forward, blocking Diane's way. 'Are you looking for something particular?' she smiles. Her voice is deep, Eastern-European, she guesses.

Diane nods. Clinique is Riona's brand. She used nothing else. 'I need everything really,' she says. The girl nods, tells her to sit up at the counter and she'll colour-match her. Diane's never been colour-matched before. 'I like what you've got on,' she tells the assistant, as the girl blends foundation on her cheeks, then stands back to examine the result. The girl nods, turns from her and moves expertly round the shelves gathering pots and sticks. 'We'll try these,' she says.

Diane enjoys the feeling of the brushes on her skin. The girl, whose name tag says Jana, leans in and tells her to blink as she holds a mascara wand dangerously close to her eye. Diane feels her breath, warm on her face, detects a faint hint of peppermint. 'Where are you from?' she asks. 'Lithuania. Have you been to Lithuania?' the girl asks. 'No.' The girl, Jana, holds the mirror before her. The transformation is complete. This time she examines her reflection and what she sees is Riona staring back at her. 'I'll take the lot,' she tells her.

In the garage, she pulls the tarpaulin from Riona's car: a red Volkswagen Beetle. She sits in, turns the key and the stereo jumps to life. George Michael croons that if he'd turned a different corner, they never would have met. It's the last song Riona listened to. She wonders if the words wormed their way into her ear, if they were there still as she walked down the seafront to the pier and through a gap in the wall to the rocks around the back. Riona.

Diane moves the car out onto the driveway. She finds a bucket and fills it with water, squirts liquid in and with a jumbo sponge from the boot she begins to wash Riona's car. Her skin sweats beneath the make-up. She's stripped down to a t-shirt when a neighbour passes, despite the cold October breeze. The woman stumbles as she nears the gate, does what in other circumstances would be a comical double-take. A small 'oh' escapes her mouth. 'Diane, for a minute I thought ...' Diane smiles. 'Hello Mrs Nolan,' she says, and then goes back to scrubbing the paintwork until it gleams.

The keys were still in the ignition when they'd found Riona's car. A mobile phone, battery dead, sat in the space before the gearbox, next to it a box containing earrings: two silver fish with diamond eyes that sparkled. Diane had charged up the phone. When she turned it on, there were eight missed calls. Four from her, two from her mother, and two from someone called JB. When she'd dialled the number and heard his voice, she didn't know what to say. Now she dials it daily and says nothing.

She hadn't felt right reading the texts; then she couldn't stop. It had been going on, it seemed, for over a year. She'd traced the words from light flirtation to clandestine arrangements, post-coital declarations, pleading, and finally bitterness. There were several messages in tandem that bore Riona's name; JB's replies became, in the end, more scattered, strained even. He'd begun to sign with his initial even though his number was saved in the phone; a formality.

In Riona's apartment, Diane showers, and empties the bag of make-up on the bed. She dials JB's number and waits for him to pick up. His voice is agitated when he does. 'Who is this?' he says. She waits. He waits too, the seconds screaming between them before she cuts the call.

A year and Riona had said nothing. Diane had spoken to Kerrie, her sister's closest friend, asked casually if Riona had been seeing anyone, if there was anyone who should know about the funeral arrangements, but Kerrie had said no. She wondered what kind of person could carry on an affair and confide in no one.

She'd tracked him down straight away, thumbed the Facebook app on Riona's phone and scrolled through her friends list: Jason Burnett. His profile picture showed him mid-air, poised for a slam on the tennis court. The only evidence that he and Riona knew each other was a group shot of the players in their gear. Riona was flushed, smiling. Her fringe clung to her forehead with sweat. They'd both been tagged, the location marked as the local club where Riona played on Tuesdays and Thursdays. Diane had clicked on his profile, but discovered nothing else. There were no pictures and he hadn't updated his status in several months either. Jason Burnett, it seemed, didn't believe in disclosure.

At 7pm, Diane opens Riona's wardrobe and pushes through the hangers. She picks out a blue wool dress and pulls it over her head. Then she sits before the bedroom mirror and carefully applies the make-up she bought. She sprays Riona's perfume, steps through the mist, and drops the bottle in her bag. She ties one of Riona's scarves round her neck, gets in the Volkswagen and drives to the club where she knows he will be. It is Thursday.

Diane pulls the car up where she can be seen by anyone exiting the club. Then she turns the ignition off, sits there and waits. It is more than half an hour before the first of the players emerge, two girls: one blonde, the other brunette. They have sports bag over their shoulders and rackets in their hands. They stand talking, unaware of Diane, not fifty metres away. The other players filter out, some alone, others in twos or threes. Jason Burnett emerges with a tall blonde girl. She recognises him right away from the picture. He smiles, says something to the girl who shakes her blonde hair and laughs, then he taps her lightly with the racket before they part. She shouts something after him, which Diane doesn't hear, and he raises the racket in salute without turning his head.

Diane watches Jason Burnette unlock a blue Audi. She commits the registration to memory before starting the engine. Then she turns the headlights on and waits for him to look up, to recognize the car. As he does so, she accelerates, tyres screeching on gravel. She drives close enough that he can glimpse her, a quick flash of her red hair before she tears out of the car park. In the rearview mirror, she sees him, motionless, staring after the Volkswagen.

About twenty minutes later, Riona's phone rings. She watches the letters JB flash on the screen until the ringing stops. She smiles when she thinks of how she must have unnerved him. The phone rings twice more during the evening, and she ignores it.

She's sitting watching television in Riona's apartment when the buzzer goes, a short, sharp sound that causes her to jump. Instinctively, she lowers the television, but the lamp is on and whoever is outside can see it through the cream curtains. She waits, heart thumping. It goes again, this time the caller leaves their finger on the buzzer, its shrill sound echoing through the apartment. Diane creeps into the bedroom, which is in darkness, closes the door behind her and lifts the edge of the curtain. Outside is the blue Audi. She draws back when she sees Jason Burnette retreat. He turns, looks up at the windows, then gets into the car and drives away.

Over the next few days, the apartment is watched. Diane sees the Audi parked across the street at night. She makes sure that she is in the apartment before he finishes work, before he can accost her in the car park and discover that she is not Riona. She sprays the bell with Riona's perfume, so that the scent will cling to his fingers should he press it; cloying and sweet.

She stops calling JB. Riona's phone, too, remains silent. After four days, the night visits stop. She looks out the window and the blue car is conspicuously absent. On the Tuesday evening, she decides to go out. She lifts the curtain to make sure that the apartment is not being watched, then she takes her bag and goes out into the night.

She is at the car when she feels a hand on her shoulder. She freezes, turns and registers the look of surprise on Jason Burnett's face. 'Did you think I was somebody else?' she says. His hand drops. The colour has risen in his face and for a moment she's afraid. She looks at the apartment block, but there is no one else around. 'Diane, I think we should talk,' he says. His voice is soft. He knows who she is, maybe he has known all along. She turns and he follows her inside.

She offers him coffee. He turns it down, then changes his mind. She feels his eyes on her as she moves around the tiny annexed kitchen. 'What did she tell you about me?' he asks. Diane fixes on him. 'Nothing,' she says. 'She never mentioned your name.' He looks at his hands. She notes how his hair is a different colour in this light, more red than mousy. She puts the mug of coffee before him, offers him milk and sugar as though he's a regular visitor, and wonders how familiar he is with this place.

'Are you married?' she asks.

He shakes his head, blows on the too-hot coffee. She is surprised by his answer. 'Girlfriend?'

JB hesitates, then nods miserably. Diane eyes him over her cup, trying to figure what attracted her sister to this man. 'What's her name, this girlfriend?'

'Annika. But look that's nothing to do with what happened ...' He puts the mug down. It makes a dull thud on the table between them.

'Oh yeah, and what was it that happened exactly?' Diane asks.

Jason Burnette stands, his chair screeching on the tiles. 'I

166

know what you're thinking,' he says. 'That I tried to end the affair and Riona couldn't take it, but that's not how it was. I didn't want it, not like that. It was her ...'

Diane stands too, she takes a few steps towards him. In heels, she's slightly taller than he is, but he looks strong, agile. 'What do you mean?' she asks. 'What was her?'

JB retreats. Her closeness, she can see, is making him nervous. 'I wanted to finish with Annika. Riona wouldn't allow it. She said if I ended it with Annika, then we were finished too. She liked the sneaking around, got a kick out of it ...'

Diane eyes JB. She thinks about the text messages on her sister's phone, of JB's lack of response. Is that why Riona had never mentioned him? It was no more than a fling, but then why the angry messages – the ones demanding that he call her back? No, she doesn't believe it.

'But you ended it anyway?' she asks.

JB nods. 'Annika got pregnant. Riona thought it was funny at first. And then she sent the picture, one of me naked in her bed ... She'd got Annika's number from my phone, decided it was time that it ended. I stopped answering her messages and she lost it, kept phoning me. I didn't want to talk to her, not after what she'd done. Annika refused to speak to me, still won't.'

Diane watches his face. 'Even if this is true,' she says. 'I'm still not seeing what it was exactly that made my sister throw herself off the pier.'

JB looks at her. 'She didn't,' he says.

'What ... Jesus, you were there?'

He opens his mouth, and then closes it. Diane moves closer. 'She called me, demanded that I meet her. At first I refused ... When I arrived, she was on the seafront waiting. She said she was sorry for what she did, but that she knew I didn't love Annika. A kid was no reason for me to stay.'

Diane watches, notes the tremor in his chin as he speaks.

In her head, she's measuring the distance to the drawer in the kitchen where the knives are kept, afraid of what it is JB will say next.

He's turned away from her. His voice is far-off in memory. *'You'd do anything for me, wouldn't you JB?* That's what she said, and I told her I would have, before I'd discovered the things she was capable of. *You would*, she said, and *I'll prove it*. She ran. I thought she was going to stop at the edge, maybe she intended to, but ...'

JB covers his mouth with his hand. Diane steps back in horror. 'You saw it,' she says. 'You were there and you fucking let her drown?' JB doesn't move as she approaches him. 'Why? She says. 'Why didn't you do something to save her?' His words are muffled, swamped by the rain of her fists on his body. He lifts his hands to stave off the blows, his words rising through a rack of sobs. 'Afraid,' he says, 'I'm afraid of the fucking water.' The sobs grow louder, and Diane doesn't know anymore if they're coming from her or from this man who she is beating.

WITNESS

When the call comes, jolting you from fractious sleep, you know it's not good. A disembodied voice, floating in darkness, tells you your father's been admitted to Tallaght Hospital, and that you should come.

As you rummage on the floor for your socks, and the dog sighs at being woken at such an ungodly hour, you think that this is what you've been waiting for, this call.

You scribble a note, detach the spare key to your flat from its keyring, and slide both beneath the door of the Polish girl that lives downstairs. She'll feed the dog, take him out for his walks. She'll bring him down to her place and sit with him watching telly until, a free man, you return.

The roads are eerie at night, a couple of taxis, plates unlit, bound for the airport is all you encounter on the motorway. Too early even for delivery trucks to be on the move. You drive below the speed limit because, apart from your groggy un-caffeinated state, you are in no hurry to get there.

You park in the multi-storey carpark, surprised by the number of cars already there, clocking up bills on the ticket machine that stands in a corner by the exit. You've always thought it wrong being charged to park in a hospital carpark. It's stealing money from sick people or from those, like you, who are about to sit vigil for god-knows-how-long; that ticket machine counting up the hours that you will never get back.

There is no one on duty at the reception desk, but the woman on the phone has told you to take the lift straight up to the second floor to the most dreaded of all wards: the intensive care unit.

You pass the shop, shutters down, inside an array of soft toys, toiletries and overpriced sandwiches that you hope not to have to purchase if the hours tick down until morning. It's bad enough you'll have to drink the rank coffee from the vending machine just to stay awake as you sit by his bedside.

You decide not to take the lift. At this hour who would be around to save you if that vast metal box were to grate to a halt between floors? Such are the thoughts that preoccupy your mind as you push open the door to the stairwell and climb the four flights of stairs that will take you to the second floor, buoyed up on nothing but the hope that he will have gone by the time you reach the locked door of the ICU ward.

You ring the bell, and a nurse comes to open the door and admit you. She is so typically a nurse, you think, in her blue uniform and thick-framed glasses. When she turns from you, and you follow her to the bedside to where your father is hooked up to an array of machines, you notice that her blonde hair, which is swept back, has been secured with nothing more than a biro.

He was found at the side of the road, she tells you. She seems embarrassed when she mentions that he was inebriated, and that he'd probably been there long enough for irreparable damage to have been done before someone stopped and called the ambulance.

You imagine him, prostrate on the footpath, passersby skirting round him, someone, a woman perhaps, insisting that they ought to stop and check that he's ok, while her partner dismisses him as a no-good drunk that'll come round in his own time. If only that woman had listened to her partner's ill advice, you might not be sitting here by your father's bedside: it might already have been over.

'He hasn't come to,' the nurse tells you. 'Is he likely to?' you ask, praying that the answer is no, that you won't have to face him after all this time, that he'll go gently, as he never did in this life. Because a gentle exit is the least that he could grant you.

It's close on six years since you last saw him. The shock of it: him turning up at your mother's funeral cuffed to a garda, as if the shame he'd brought on the family wasn't enough. You'd walked straight past his outstretched hand as though he were a ghost in the aisle. Felt the discomfort of those standing in the pews near him.

You add it up and calculate that he'd be sixty seven now. You're amazed he's lasted this long with his lifestyle when your poor mother was taken at only fifty nine. That was the last time you'd had to visit this hospital, and you still remember it clear as day. The consultant calling you into that small room and telling you that she might still rally, that she might pull through, and then that same evening, that young nurse telling you that if she were you, she'd stay. And something in her tone made up your mind for you. And you lay vigil on a cramped camp bed watching your mother in the semi-dark until she breathed her last, and the first thing you felt was relief that her battle was over.

Now you listen to your father's breath, the dull pump of oxygen through the mask forcing him to inhale. A massive heart attack, she said. And you almost told her you didn't think he'd had a heart to fail – or that if he had, it was the blackness of that heart that had finally caught up with him, but instead you nodded and said nothing. You didn't even question how they'd got your number.

It's difficult to know if he's changed – physically that is. The mask covers most of his face, his bulk looks the same – not the emaciated state that people often describe beneath the thin hospital-standard blanket. His hands lay palms down by his sides. Those same hands that you know have caused so much hurt; that your mother, when she found out, couldn't bear to have touch her.

When you look at these hands now you expect to see some sign – something ugly that will brand them – but instead the nails are clipped short, they are shaped, maybe even manicured, not a speck of dirt beneath them. But then you remember, he was always fastidious about his appearance. The dirt only ever lurked on the inside.

You didn't know what was going on – at least that was what you told yourself. You thought your father's eagerness was down to the fact that you'd finally made a friend, someone to invite over to the house, even if that someone was a girl. It made you less strange – a bit of a Nancy boy maybe, that was what he called you when he wanted to hurt you. 'But sure no harm,' he told your mother on his good days, 'he'll grow out of that.'

You weren't a gregarious kid and truth be told you were happy enough on your own most of the time. The kids at school thought you were weird, you knew that, but somehow that didn't bother you.

You hadn't wanted to invite Alice Spencer home in the first place. She'd invited herself, insisted she walk you home because she was bigger than you, and when your father had invited her in and given you both red lemonade and biscuits, it seemed she decided to latch on to you. And she wasn't that bad really – if you didn't mind the assertive sort, which you didn't.

The blonde-haired nurse comes to check on your father. There's something about her that reminds you of Alice Spencer, the woman she turned out to be when you saw her again standing in the witness box, some fifteen years later. Maybe it's the glasses, you think, or the way she looks at you with something like veiled sympathy – which was unexpected given the circumstances. You watch the nurse lay her hand gently on your father's perfectly manicured one, and you wonder if she'd still do that if she knew – if she'd even entertain the idea of keeping this man alive. You know you wouldn't.

Alice's message had come as a shock. She'd tracked you down in the phone book, written you a letter. She told you that she'd made contact with some other young women from the old neighbourhood, that they were building a case against your father. She said she knew it was difficult, that she wanted you to know that she didn't blame you, but more importantly, that you were an eyewitness.

You didn't answer right away. But then you did. You wanted to know who the others were.

They come to you now with the buzz from the fluorescent light over the nurse's station – the names of the girls you'd never met until that day in court, but that have stayed with you. You hadn't been able to meet the eye of those young women, even as you stood in the witness box and confirmed what you'd seen, taking their side against your father. You couldn't bear the fact that they knew that you were the offspring of such a monster.

You'd only seen it once. You'd been out in the tree house your father had bought, and he'd sent you in for more lemonade. But you'd come back quicker than he thought because you couldn't open the bottle because the cap was sticky with sugar. Your father had been angry then, called you a pansy. 'You're useless,' he said. 'Can you do nothing boys do?' He drove Alice home then – took the bag of sweets he'd given you both to share and pushed them into her hands.

You didn't question why it took him an hour to return when Alice lived ten minutes away. But you did notice that Alice didn't seem to want to come over to your house to play anymore – that she had no appetite for the bags of sweets your father gave her.

The last call you'd got about your father was when he was being released from prison. They asked if you'd come to collect him, if you'd be willing to help him adjust to the outside world. You'd refused to get involved, told them rather shortly that you had every confidence that the prison services would do an ample job. What did they expect? You hadn't once been to see him.

A machine starts up an erratic blip, and you look up. The nurse mistakes your hopeful look for concern; she thumbs a wheel on the tube to release water from the drip and tells you it's nothing. She smiles to reassure you.

Hours pass and nothing happens. You listen to the whirring of the machines and the occasional blip – the snores of a patient two beds up who occasionally jolts himself awake only to settle into the same rhythm seconds later. You drink cup after cup of bad coffee from the vending machine, and you ask yourself what you're doing here – although you already know the answer. If he wakes, you think, you will walk out of here. You will descend the same stairs you climbed a few hours earlier, pay for your ticket at the machine that's clocking up your wasted hours, and you will drive home as the dawn breaks and wait until the next time. You have come here to see an end to it. You have come here to bury your father.

Many thanks to the editors of journals where versions of these stories have appeared:

'Death's Child', 'Mongo' and 'The Dare' were all published in *Crannóg*; 'Storms' was first published in *Empty House: Poetry and Prose on the Climate Crisis* (Doire); 'Between the Lines' was published in *Southword* 39; 'The Driver' and 'After Ada' appeared in *The Lonely Crowd*; A flash version of 'After Ada' appeared in *Impspired* as did 'Ding Dong Johnny' and 'Ashes'; 'Incendiary' was published in *Bray Arts Journal*.

Special thanks to publisher Alan Hayes for his unparalleled support of Irish writers. And to Dave who is always the first to read my work. Huge gratitude to Mike McCormack, Rosemary Jenkinson and John O'Donnell for their very kind comments on this collection. Thanks also to: Antoinette, Adrianna, Keith, David and Eamon for their enduring friendship. And to my writer friends: Edward and Eamon Mc who have read many of these stories. Special thanks to BeRn whose song 'No Star Lesbian' inspired the story of the same name. This story is also inspired, in part, by the poet Anne Walsh Donnelly.

This collection is dedicated to my dear friend Keith Evans. And to Liam, David, and Wayne Marc *x*

Tanya Farrelly is the author of three previous books: her debut, *When Black Dogs Sing* (Arlen House, 2016), a short fiction collection which was longlisted for the Edge Hill Short Story Prize and won the Kate O'Brien Award 2017, and two novels: *The Girl Behind the Lens* (2016) and *When Your Eyes Close* (2018), both from Harper Collins. She holds a Ph.D. in Creative and Critical Writing from Bangor University, Wales, and teaches at numerous institutions, including the Irish Writers Centre, Dublin, and the People's College. She is the founder and director of Bray Literary Festival and was appointed Writer in Residence at NUI Galway in 2021.